Jorkens Remembers Africa

Lord Dunsany

West Martian Limited Company
1st Edition, October 2024

First printing 2024
The publisher can be contacted at westmartian.com
ISBN-13: 9798330480791 Paperback

Contents

Preface

It may perhaps be pointed out by some of my readers that Jorkens Remembers Africa is a title that does not apply to all of these tales. And yet it is to the deserts and forests of Africa that Jorkens' memory seems to return the most gladly, whenever I or any other friend have been so happy as to awaken it to its true brilliance by our little trifling gifts. Many a man's memory as he grows old loses slowly its colour and splendour, till pictures that he believed could never fade, fall from it one by one. How fortunate if the refreshments that we sometimes offer Jorkens are able to open again that closed but brilliant inner eye, till we watch it gazing once more steadfast and child-like sheer in the face of Truth.

Jorkens Remembers Africa

The Lost Romance

All through the summer Jorkens had told us no story. He often lunched at the Billiards Club, but it was never his custom to talk much while he was eating, and afterwards he used to rest in a chair. I would not say he slept; it was rather more of a torpor; and, although he muttered sometimes, he told no story. Nobody minded; there are all sorts of things to do in summer: gardening, golf, weeding lawns, and a hundred other things that take up one's time and one's interest and give one plenty to talk about, without needing to listen to Jorkens. I recollect one member of our club telling me a story about gardening. It was not in the least true, but it served to pass the time away and entitled one to tell a similar tale in return. Then someone else would talk of his garden, and so on. And all the while Jorkens lay undisturbed in his chair. But when November came, when gardening was over, when the days grew short in London almost suddenly, and the fog and the night began to shut down upon us in earnest, then it hardly seemed that any tales we might tell could bring back to our memories any ray of lost summer, and some of us naturally turned to Jorkens then; for, whatever we may think of the method he had of inspiring himself, his tales had at any rate an origin in lands that shimmered with sunshine, and he seemed to have the knack of bringing some of it to us through the dark and early evening that hung bleak by our windows. So one November day, quite early in the month, I took the liberty of talking to Jorkens while he rested after his lunch; and though he did not immediately recall who I was, or follow the trend of my remarks, I certainly brought back his attention to us, so that later on when another of us referred to one or two of his earlier gallantries, a twinkle woke in his eye, though he did not speak. He did not speak until he had had some refreshment that I was only too glad to provide for him; and then I questioned him directly. I had framed my question with some care, knowing that the unusual had an unfailing attraction for Jorkens. "Have you ever failed," I asked, "in any affair with a lady?"

For a moment he seemed about to say "No," when the banality of such an answer froze the word on his lips, and for several seconds he appeared deep in thought.

"Only once," said Jorkens. "No, only once. Oh, it is a long time ago now, and it was a long long way from here. I'll tell you. It was in the island of Anaktos. You probably don't know it, in the Mediterranean, far away from here. In the Mediterranean in the early summer. Well, it's all gone now. But that summer in Anaktos I first saw her, walking along a path under the pepper trees in the bright morning. There were eighteen of them, sisters of the Greek Reformed Church. They had a convent on the island, and it was easy to see where she came from; that was not the difficulty. The difficulty was in speaking to her at all, or in even seeing her face. Yes, they don't wear cowls, those sisters; they veil themselves completely. They wear white gloves too: you don't see an inch of skin. They have some sort of holy saying that where a fly can alight there is room for Satan. Well, there it was, you see. And yet, for all that, I got the idea, and never have I had any idea more strongly, that she was extraordinarily beautiful. She was tall and slender and she had lovely hands, and she walked with a stride as graceful and light as the step of any young antelope, slipping unseen from the forest on hooves unheard by the lions. Of her hair I can tell you nothing, and I never saw her eyes.

"She walked third on the left, of the eighteen. It was a difficult situation: I was determined to speak to her alone; and you can do that even when they are walking with seventeen others, if once you can catch their eye; but when you cannot even see their eyes, you cannot make any sign to one more than to the whole lot. Even if I waited at a corner and signed just as she came round . . . no, there seemed no way of doing it. Oh, I did a lot of thinking. I thought of leaving a note in the path, with a leaf over it, and pulling the leaf away with a bit of silk just as the second two passed it, and it would be right before her. She always walked in the same place in that procession. But that would have been no use, because they would have all seen her stoop to pick it up, and I knew where that note would have gone. I somehow felt sure when I first saw the procession that it would come the same way every day at the same hour, except of course on saints' days; and, sure enough, it did. And every day my belief in her surpassing beauty grew stronger, and for a week I could think of nothing that was any good at all. They'd a good wall at the convent; quite ten feet high, and broken glass on the top that didn't look to me particularly Christian. But it wasn't the wall that stopped me, but the impossibility of finding her if I got over, before I found one of the others, or nine of them for that matter, for that's what the odds were. If I threw a note over, the odds were no better; and of course I didn't even know her name.

"Well, at the end of the week the idea came to me. Of course all great ideas are simple ones; but I'd been thinking too hard, and so I hadn't hit on it. And when it did come I can take no credit for it: I didn't get it by thinking. I was walking to a place, a little wood, where I could be alone and think things out, one day when she had passed me for the seventh or eighth time, with that gentle and beautiful stride, her hands swaying very softly like slightly wind-blown flowers; I was pushing into the wood, which nobody owned or tended, when a burr stuck to my clothes. I doubt if I should ever have found any way to speak to her, if it had not been for that. I had barely touched the burr and yet it stuck; and when I tried to pull it off it seemed to stick harder than ever.

"That's what I got my idea from. And what I did was to write a note on tissue paper and roll it up very small and fasten it on to the burr. I simply wrote, 'Most beautiful of the sisters, here or in any land; I must speak with you. Tell me where to come. If you refuse, be sure that I shall, go to everlasting perdition.'

"I didn't set much store by the last sentence, because after all she was a woman. But just in case she was too much frozen by dogma, then the threat of hell would be just the thing for her; because it is their job to keep souls from hell, not to send them there. So I threw that in on the tiny bit of paper. Practically blackmail.

"Well, I never quite knew which part of the letter fetched her, but some part of it did. For I walked towards them along their path next day and threw the burr at her dress as she passed; and, not the day following that, but the day after that one, the same burr hit my jacket as we passed at the usual place. Her note said 'At five tomorrow in our orchard, if you can climb the wall by the ilex.'

"If I could climb the wall. Five stone less than I am now, and invisible wings to lift me; that's what one has in youth. Yes, I could climb the wall. I made a sort of ladder for the near side, out of logs, and took up plenty of sacking for the glass bottles. Then I fastened a rope to the trunk of a handy tree and took the end over the wall with me to get back by. The ilex was no use for climbing down, but it was a world of use for concealing me from the windows. And there was the orchard underneath me, and plenty of cover from the trees if you went carefully. She was standing there expecting me, and looking pretty grim, so far as you could tell by her attitude; to make up, I almost fancied, for her lapse in answering my note. Why, even reading it, in a place like that, was probably more of a sin than shoplifting would be here. Well, there she stood, looking pretty forbidding, but it was her all right; there could be no doubt of that, though her face was still muffled up and gloves covered her hands and wrists.

"Her first words to me were: 'Why did you write that you would go to everlasting perdition? What did you mean by it?'

"'Because,' I said, 'your beauty has so profoundly enchanted me.'

"'How can you know,' she asked, 'if I am beautiful or not?'

"And I was so enthralled by a strange certainty that I answered: 'I know.'

"And then she went back to her original question, 'Why everlasting perdition?'

"'Because,' I said, 'there would be nothing else left for me.'

"'But how?' she asked.

"'Easy enough,' I said. 'Just helplessly drifting.'

"She wouldn't leave that point for a long while. But I didn't want to talk about my soul. I had better things to talk of. You know how it is if you're with a beautiful woman, and she is all wrapped up in mystery; you don't think much about your soul. But she didn't want to talk of anything else. I began to wish I had never mentioned it. And yet, if I hadn't, who knows if I'd ever have seen her. I thought at first that I had attracted the woman in her, and that she was only pretending to be more interested in everlasting perdition. But she stuck to her point until I began to wonder. And such a place for a talk like that; the grey boles of old apple trees clustered in a quiet angle of the great convent wall, the green lawns flashing beyond through gaps in the gnarled branches, with the old ilex shadowing us and sheltering us from view. What a place for a talk about Hell! But she would have it. And I would have it that it was to Hell I would go if her beauty took no pity on me.

"Again, 'How do you know if I am beautiful?'

"And again I swore to her in all sincerity that I surely knew she was lovely.

"And then she ridiculed me; and then my turn came. 'Take off those veils,' I said. 'And prove it.'

"And at first she said 'No,' and that it was against the rules of their Order. But I said, 'No. You have mocked at truth. You laughed at me for saying that you were beautiful. Truth comes before all your rules.'

"I argued like that with her for a while, and at last I saw I was winning. She hadn't said she would unveil, but I knew she was going to; I was as sure as one sometimes is that some bursting bud in Spring, on an early morning, will be an open flower by noon. Her hands moved to her hood where all those veils were fastened, then she let them drop again and began to talk of her childhood. Who she was and what she was she did not say, but she spoke of a terror that came when she was young, moving from village to village as quietly as lengthening shadows, and bringing death with it or life-long disfigurement: that was the smallpox. 'I was perhaps,' she said, and seemed to tremble as though Satan would hear her, 'perhaps I was beautiful then.'

"'And what, what happened then?' I asked as well as I could, for something came to me suddenly, like an icy wind through the apple-trunks, a fear, for the first time, of something amiss.

"'The smallpox,' she said simply. 'I just escaped with my life. Of my beauty' (and still she said the word as though it were sin to speak it) 'nothing remained, and scarcely even my features.'

"'Scarcely . . .' I blurted out, and found no more to say. And she kindly filled the gap in our shattered conversation.

"'You do not wish to see my face now?' she said.

"But that was not true. I could have wept to hear of the ruin of that beauty of which I felt so sure. And yet I could not believe that in the ruins was no trace at all of the radiant face I had fancied. And fancy wasn't the word for it either: it seemed nothing less than insight.

"So I said, 'Yes. Still. And as much as ever.'

"I thought that the glory that is in beautiful faces might linger there even yet.

"And then to console her for whatever was lost, and because it was perfectly true, I said: 'You have a beautiful voice.'

"And she answered: 'All my people have beautiful voices.'

"And as yet she had said nothing of who they were.

"'Your people?' I said.

"'Yes, the Hottentots,' was her answer.

"'The Hottentots!' I exclaimed.

"And she seemed offended by something she heard in my voice, and repeated proudly, 'The Hottentots.'

"Did I tell you we were speaking in English, and perfect English?

"'But you speak English,' I gasped.

"'The English rule there,' she said.

"'But the convent! The Order?' I blurted out, clinging still to a despairing hope that what she told was impossible.

"'It is open to all,' she said, 'accepting the discipline of the Greek Reformed Church.'

"I was silent, silent, silent. You could hear the young leaves swaying to a small breeze lost in the apple trees. And then after a long while she spoke again. She turned her veiled face to me, I remember, and said: 'You still wish to see my face?'

"And I said 'Yes.' What else could one say? I could hardly say No, even if I hadn't asked her to unveil. When I said Yes, she moved her hands again to her hood and began the untying of a great number of knots, and all of them seemed as tight as though some elder hand had wrenched them shut with a jerk. It gave my eyes time to rove, and my thoughts with them. Otherwise I should have seen her face. But now I saw, far enough off, I admit, but I saw two sisters walking over a lawn: I saw their white dresses every now and then as they crossed the little vistas between the trunks of the apple-trees. And I meant to tell her this, and to say that if unveiling was against the rules of her convent, now would not be the time to do it. But her hands were busy with the last of those knots. And all I said in the end was, 'Perhaps not now.'

"Then I took one long long look at her, remembering my illusion, an illusion that is often with me still, coming suddenly back to me at a glimpse of orchards or ilex; then I went to my rope and got back over the wall."

And Jorkens looked sadly into the deeps of the fire, as though the old illusion were glowing there still and a little warming the blood of the middle-aged man by its beauty, after Lord knows how long. In common gratitude I signed to the waiter.

Really there was no more for anyone to say. Watley needn't have spoken at all. And yet he did. And this was what he said: "It was no illusion, Jorkens."

"What!" said Jorkens.

"No illusion," Watley repeated. "The sisters of the Greek Reformed Church are the loveliest girls in those islands. They make a point of it. Whenever they get a beautiful girl they count it a victory over Satan. And they are beautiful."

"But a Hottentot," said Jorkens, "disfigured by smallpox."

"Oh, that," said Watley with a wave of his hand as though sweeping smallpox and Hottentot out of the world. "They keep their wits about them. 'Be cunninger than the Tempter' is one of their mottoes."

Jorkens gripped the whiskey that was by now beside him, and drained it without a word. Again I signed to the waiter. Still Jorkens was utterly silent, and seemingly miles away from us, or more likely years and years. Another whiskey came, and he drained that too. And as he still said nothing, sitting there heedless of us, we went quietly away from the room and left him alone. As I went through the door he still seemed searching and searching for something lost in the sinking glow of the fire.

The Curse of the Witch

The talk had veered round to runes and curses and witches, one bleak December evening, where a few of us sat warm in easy chairs round the cheery fire of the Billiards Club.

"Do you believe in witches?" one of us said to Jorkens.

"It isn't what I believe in that matters so much," said Jorkens; "only what I have seen."

"Have you seen one?" the other man asked.

"I know how they work," he said.

"And how do they work?" we asked him.

"Well," Jorkens said, "I want to be strictly accurate. I had once a fairly good glimpse of how one of them worked, but I can't say more than that. Different witches in different countries may perhaps have various methods. And yet I doubt it: I imagine they travel more than we suppose, and meet and talk many things over. Many a blackened patch under a hedgerow may have been a meeting place for queer discussions, and the comparing of strange notes. But who knows? Who knows?"

And somehow I feared that Jorkens was about to drift from the particular to the general, and though he might have had much to say on that that could have been instructive, yet we should have got no story. "You met a witch once, Jorkens?" I asked.

"I didn't meet her," said Jorkens. "She had probably been dead three hundred years when I chanced upon her locality. But I certainly met something of her work."

And without any further stimulus of any sort from me he gave us his story. "It's a curious thing, when I was young," he said, "there used to come on me at times an instinct such as some birds have. Swallows I mean, corncrakes, cuckoos and all those. I felt driven southwards, felt that I must migrate. So one day I started South, and kept on till I came to Spain, walking mostly. All through France, and on foot through the Pyrenees. And one day I came to a village that somehow seemed right. Nothing there jarred on me, the roofs of the small houses comforted me, quaint chimneys seemed to beckon; little old doorways looked as though in a moment that was almost trembling to come, they would break into wooden green smiles. Over it hung the lazy sunshine of Spring, on which hawks balanced lightly, and whither went up the sound of bells from below. It almost seemed to be roofed and sheltered by sunlight and fading vibrations of bells, interlaced in a dome. That's how it seemed to me, and something at once soothed my restlessness, and I went to an inn and stayed. Probably the roofs of barns in some quiet valley have the same hold on a wandering swallow. One can't say what it is.

"The inn was of course uncomfortable, I didn't mind that; the only thing I minded was that as the night went on, and a large moon rose and I wanted to get to sleep, the most infernal howling of dogs began. The room that I had been given by the old couple that owned the inn looked out from the edge of the village over a lonely moorland, and a mile away over the hills and hollows of this wild country I could see the black shape of a large house, from which the melancholy up-roar came. I could not have believed that it was so far, for the sound seemed almost underneath my window, but the old inn-keeper that showed me up to my room said, at the first howl, 'The hounds in the Casa Viljeros.' And he pointed with his hand out of the window to the dark shape of the house. I asked no more about it then, for my curios-ity had not been aroused and excited; it sounded no more at first than the ordinary baying of hounds that are a little disturbed or uneasy be-fore they sleep; and so the old man left me and went downstairs and I knew no more than the name of the dark house where there were hounds. Through sleepless hours while the baying of these hounds rose into long howls, I wished a hundred times that I had questioned him, as far as my Spanish would go. There was a horror in knowing nothing. Even the strange story I got next day, perhaps even the whole story, which I shall never know, might have made that night less hor-rible. It was hearing those cries going up from some terror of which I knew nothing, that made it worse than if I had known the cause. For it was from some terror that those hounds were howling; one af-ter another they spoke with little uneasy yelps, drawn out at last into one long wavering howl. Had it been human beings shouting a mile away one could not have heard their words, and might well have been in the dark as to what they debated among them; but those that have not any words in their language are not to be so mistaken, and their tones when they speak are as clear to Englishman or to Spaniard as to whatever roves on soft feet through open moors in the night. So there I sat all night listening to terror, and never knowing what the terror was. It was no use trying to sleep, for it was not only the noise that kept me awake: had words that I could not understand been shouted, however close, I should have got to sleep in time. But when one's understanding is involved, when one knows the message but knows not why it is sent, then wonder awakes and all one's mind is active. At first in the silence that followed the long howls I thought they had finished and that the terror was over; but always as soon as a few seconds had passed a low whimper would come quavering over the moor, then another, and then another a little louder, and then again the long cry burdened with terror. Separate voices at first, and I even tried to count them; but an hour or so after midnight, as though their forebodings had gathered force and accumulated, the yelps and whimperings all drew together, and rippled into a howl in which every voice was wailing. Nothing stirred on the grey moor, nobody entered or left the dark house; the hounds howled on and on, voicing their fear of a mystery to which I had no key. And even when dawn at last lifted a little of the weight of foreboding, by changing the shape of the scene over which it had brooded so long, bringing hills into view that one had not seen before, and taking away a frown from the faces of others; even then the terrified hounds, though weary of howling, were whimpering mournfully in the early light.

"What was it? What was that terror of which they told so unmistakably? Before bright morning came I may have slept a little; however that be, as soon as the old man called me, and afterwards as I had breakfast with him and his wife, I asked him for all he could tell of the house called Casa Viljeros; and on the evening of the same day I talked to the Americans who had bought the house, sitting for an hour with them over a few cocktails at the hotel in the town ten miles away, and getting from them pretty well all they knew; and I talked a bit with the gardener at the house; I got everybody's story except that of the Viljeros family, who from the old Marquis downwards would say never a word. And from all I heard I put this tale together.

"Nobody knew the age of Casa Viljeros. It was not like an English house, of which people say Queen Anne, Queen Elizabeth, or King Stephen: nobody knew. And the family of Viljeros was far older than the house. Their grand old motto stood out in stone over the door, 'Never the Moors.' It meant that the Moors should never hold Spain; and whatever topic the family might discuss, especially if they talked of the Government's policy, as they sometimes did in the evening, the old Marquis nearly always brought it round to that policy of his family, often ending the discussion for the night with the very words of the motto. And the time came, so the gardener said, when all the money was gone. The Marquis had little concerned himself with it when it was there, and could hardly believe it was not there: the wealth of a hidalgo seemed too natural to boast of, even in thought, and too much a part of his natural state to be gone while he still lived. And yet it was gone.

"But that his very house should go, and such a house as Casa Viljeros, was to him so utterly terrible, that he did not sell it as other men sell their houses, showing which is the key of the front door and which the key of the cellar, but kept one thing untold.

"And the Americans came, the family of Stolger. The business must have been done mostly by letter, for when first the gardener saw them they came into the house and the old family went out after little more than an hour. There were six of them, Gateward Stolger and his wife, Hendrik the eldest son, about twenty-five, two daughters and Easel, a boy of about sixteen. They all walked into the house; and there was the old Marquis, still there with his daughters, clinging to the home to the very last moment. Gateward Stolger had once seen the house from the outside, years ago on a holiday; but none of the Stolgers had ever been inside it. The money had been paid and the queer hurried bargain concluded, and nothing remained to be done but to show the new owners the way upstairs, and to tell them which was the boudoir and which was the library, and one other thing, that was never told them. The Stolgers had bought it lock, stock and barrel; furniture, sheets and everything; and had the idea of hunting there during the winter, and had brought their own hounds with them, the hounds I heard.

"And so the old hidalgo showed them round, with a great sombre politeness. They went from room to room; and, whatever glamour was hoarded there for the ancient Spanish family, the Americans saw none they would care to sit in till they came to the great library. Against this they could say nothing, indeed for some moments they could not speak at all; that splendid piece of the past merely held them spellbound. Evening was coming on and the room was dim: down the middle of the long room you saw the gloaming, and on either side the darkness of old carved wood and great shadows; it passed through the mind of one of them that they looked on a piece of the very history of Spain set in a strange darkness. One more room the old Marquis showed them, and that was all. And then the eldest of his two daughters spoke to him. 'Won't you tell them about . . . ?' she said.

"'Oh, yes,' he said at once, 'the laundry.' And he began to tell the Americans where that was; and the daughter said no more; and yet there remained an expectancy on her face, a listening to every word that her father said, a hope each time he spoke that he was about to tell the new owners what she wanted. They all went out into the old walled garden then, and it was on one of its narrow paths while passing by a clump of old boles of quince, among which the gardener was working (as much as he ever did), that the Marquis dropped behind and said to his daughter: 'All that it is necessary for him to know about the house I shall tell him.'

"And she said, 'But, Father, you must tell him about the curse.'

"'No,' he said in such a way that she might have seen that further words were useless, 'we have borne it for ten generations, so they can now.'

"'We!' she said. 'But we are of steel, steel of Toledo. How will they ever . . .' but he would have no more of it: he was hit too hard by the loss of Casa Viljeros to be capable of ordinary right sympathies; and his daughter saw that she could do nothing more for the strangers that were so light-heartedly entering her home. And the other daughter dared say nothing at all. If any more was said there is no trace of it.

"That evening with the last of the light the Viljeros family lumbered away in a wonderful old carriage, and the Americans entered the house with a few servants, and the hounds arrived and were well enough housed in the stables.

"They had dinner cheerily enough, but for the gradual approach of a certain uneasiness; and then they went to sit in the long library, which was lighted now by nearly a gross of candles. For a little while they walked round the room, looking at the faces of the satyrs carved on great chests and cupboards, and wondering what romances slept through the ages wrapped in their blackened leather along the shelves. But soon they found that they were going on tip-toe, and knew from this that they were offending against the hush, and sat down and spoke in whispers. They seemed to think that, if they sat still for a while, the silence brooding among the shadows would pass. Yet it was far otherwise, for the frowns on the faces of the satyrs seemed rather to increase in grimness, and every shadow that slipped from its place as a candle flickered began to look like a warning. And when Easel went out and got twenty or thirty more candles, the shadows that were driven further away seemed only to gather together with grimmer intent in the corners. Soon it seemed they were boding something, seemed that whenever you caught one of the dark corners with the tail of your eye it was threatening you, a warning you only lost when you looked straight at it. Look straight at it then, the reader may say. But which was right, the straight gaze or the tail of the eye? And while you looked straight at one sinister shadow, there were dozens more all round that went on with their warnings. They spoke little of all this, scarce spoke at all, all waiting for the strangeness of the house, as they called it, to go away; but nothing material or immaterial left that house after the old hidalgo and his daughters had rocked away down the road in their wonderful carriage. Here they were in the long library with whatever the ages had given to that dark house: travellers across the Atlantic might come and go, but the mystery of Casa Viljeros kept house with its own communion of shadows. As the candles burned lower imperceptible changes occurred in the shadow assembly; some grew taller, some blacker, but one and all seemed to grow, and the whole room with them, more menacing, more foreboding, more sure of a doom. They got fresh candles and the three men carried them all over the room, sending the darker shadows scurrying away from their lurking-places; they had done it to cheer the women, and to show they were not afraid, but the leaping shadows driven from their old corners brought anything but cheer, and all the Stolger family knew that things were going badly with their new possession if it had come already to showing they were not afraid. And very soon they came back to their chairs and all moved closer together; and the shadows slipped back to their places and the menace was deeper yet.

"Had they spoken they knew that things would have been better, that the echoes of their own voices might have been stronger than whatever it was that they would not yet put a name to; and this they tried to do, but by now they were all of them speaking only in whispers. They should have spoken out, they should have shouted, they should have told stale jokes or sung common songs, and they might have set up some sort of a rampart from scraps of the twentieth century to hold back this ancient thing, whatever it was, that was filling the room with terror; but they spoke in whispers, and that dark influence came at them right down the ages. And hour by hour it grew in intensity. I suppose they were afraid to go to bed. Midnight found them still there, sitting all close together, and the menace of the unknown influence deeper. Easel, the youngest, had at one time drawn his revolver, but the moment he did it he saw himself what a childish act it was; the revolver looked so sharp of outline and shiny among the vague forms of those threatening shadows. And the leers seemed to deepen upon the lips of the satyrs. With the flare of a candle, with the sudden turn of an eye, a few letters of faded gilt would light up now and then on the back of some sombre book, half a word of Spanish whispering without meaning out of the years that were troubling them, and blinking away with its warning all untold.

"A few more candles had been collected now and then, until they saw that by multiplying candles they only multiplied shadows, and that there was something more in the gloom than what could be driven away by a few of these little flames. They saw too, or felt or knew, that whatever darkness the candles drove back from the little circle in which they sat huddled together only lurked just out of sight behind some edge of old timber, waiting to stalk out upon them as soon as the candles dwindled, surely and swiftly in all the majesty of their darkness.

"It was not the dwindling of the candles, it was not any fading of the light from their flames, that brought a great change after midnight; it was something that lay in the very shadows themselves, something that earlier in the night had been dormant, or not ascertainable by human emotions, and that was now active and stirring and not to be overlooked by human fears. Against this terror they did nothing further now, carried no more candles about, drew out no more youthful revolvers, but recognized themselves in the grip of some influence against which such things were idle. And the curse, for such it was, gloomed, multiplied and foreboded; and there they sat, a little castaway group, lost as though the twentieth century had suddenly foundered, amidst an encroaching power from an age of which they knew nothing.

"What were they to do? As the night went on the curse grew stronger and darker, as though the witch that had anciently laid it upon that house were forcing it down on it with both hands, mass upon mass of it out of dark and dangerous air; while out of the shadows rose up those oaken satyrs larger than man, with scorn on their carven lips. What could they do if they daren't leave that little circle in which they sat close together in the brightest part of the room, and daren't speak louder than whisperings? More and more ominous grew the shadows. And then Hendrik speaking out loud said to his father: 'Look here, Dad, I've travelled in South America; I know magic when I see it. And I've seen something of witchcraft. There's a curse here, in this room; there's no doubt of it.'

"They all started a bit at that. And Hendrik went on. 'Well, I'm only putting it into words,' he said. 'Don't you all feel it?'

"They had nothing to say to that: they could not say it was not so.

"'Let's take the car over to Hurgos,' he said. 'They've an hotel there called the Annunciation. Let's live there. And let's start now.'

"And at that moment the hounds, that were never quite easy in their new kennels, gave tongue at the moon. And Hendrik went on: 'Let's keep the hounds in here, to show them what we think of their Spanish curses.'

"'In the library?' said his father.

"And all Hendrik answered was: 'They ought to have told us there was something wrong about the damned place.'

"'But why should it affect us?' said his father.

"'Well, doesn't it?' said Hendrik.

"And that they found unanswerable.

"With one man speaking his mind and the rest only whispering, you can easily guess how it went. 'We can come over whenever we want,' Hendrik explained. 'It mayn't be so bad by day.'

"They went there and then. And they turned the hounds into the library as Hendrik had said.

"Why the witch laid that curse all those ages ago I never enquired of the gardener, nor what exactly it was. But I felt I knew something of it myself, though it could not be put into words, from listening to those hounds all night in the library. Something was there that they knew of and told to the night, and too much book-learning and living in towns had blunted my ears to the sense of it. It was something that . . . but no words of mine can make it clear to you now. You should have heard those hounds a mile away over the moor, howling, howling, howling."

The Pearly Beach

We could not remember, any of us at the Club, who it was that first invented the twopenny stamp on cheques. There were eight or nine of us there, and not one of us could put a name to him. Of course a lot of us knew, but we'd all forgotten it. And that started us talking of the tricks memory plays. Some said memory didn't matter so much; some said it was looking forward that mattered most in business, or even watching closely what was going on around you now. And at that Jorkens stepped in. No, memory was the thing, he said; he could have made more by a good steady memory than by any amount of looking into the future.

"I don't see how that could be," said a stock-broker, who had just bought Jaffirs at 62, on pretty good information that they would go to 75. As a matter of fact they fell to 59¼.

But Jorkens stuck to his point. "With a good all-round memory," he said, "I could have made millions."

"But how?" asked the stock-broker.

"Well, it was this way," said Jorkens. "I had a rather nice pearl in a tie-pin. And things weren't quite going the way I liked; financially, I mean. Well, to cut a long story short, I decided to pop my pearl. I remember waiting till it was dark one winter's evening, so as to get to the pawnshop decently unobserved. And I went in and unscrewed the pearl off its pin, and saw it no more. That put the financial position on a sound basis again; but I came out a little what you call ruefully, and I suppose my face must have shown it, and I was sticking back what was left of my gold pin into my tie. Funny how anyone could have noticed all that, but I've observed that when people are a little bit drunk they sometimes do. Anyway there was a tall man leaning against a wall, a man I had never seen before in my life, and he looked at me in a lazy sort of way, not troubling to move his head, only his eyes, and even them he seemed barely troubling to turn and keep open; and he said, 'You want to go to Carrapaccas beach. That's where you want to go.' And he gave me the latitude and longitude. 'Pearls to be had for the gathering there,' he said.

"And I asked him what he meant, why he spoke to me. I asked him all kinds of things. But all he would say was, 'You go to Carrappas beach,' not even giving it the same name the second time.

"Well, I jotted the latitude and longitude down on my shirt-cuff;

both shirt-cuffs, to be quite sure; and I thought the thing over a lot. And the first thing I saw as I thought things over was that the man was perfectly genuine; he had probably had this secret for years, and then one day he had had a drop too much, and had blurted the thing out. You may say what you like against drink, but you don't find a man to tell you a thing like that, just because he's sorry for you for losing a pearl, when he's sober. And mind you the Carrappas beaches, or whatever he called them, were there. The longitude was a long way East, and the latitude a lot South, and I started one day from London, heading for Aden. Did I tell you all this was in London? No place like it for starting on journeys. Well, I started from London and came again to Aden. I had a very curious romance there once. In fact I was married in Aden. Well, well, that's all gone now.

"So I came to Aden and began looking about. What I was looking for was three sailors; I fancied we could do it with that; and one of those queer small boats with green keels. Sails, of course. Well, I found two sailors; just the men I was looking for. One was named Bill, and the other The Portugee, though both looked English to me so far as I could tell. And they could get another man who was a half-wit, who they said would do very well. The beauty of that was that only two had to be in it. I told them at once it was something to do with treasure, and they said that the third hand could be left on board when the rest of us went ashore, and would be quite happy singing a song that he sang. I never knew what his name was; Bill and the Portugee used just to shout at him, and he would always answer. His home was Aden; I never learned where the other two came from. Well, I told Bill the latitude and the longitude, and we slipped out in a tiny ship one morning from Aden, sailing towards India. And it was a long, long time before we came to Carrappas beach, or whatever it was. And day after day the sky was the same blistering blue, till sunset flamed in our faces, gazing back over the stern, and there came every evening behind us the same outburst of stars, and all the way the half-wit sang the same song; only the sea altered. And at last we got there, as Bill had promised we would, a tiny bay with a white beach shining, shut off by rocks from the rest of the coast, and from the inner land by a cliff, a low cliff steep behind it. The little bay was no more than fifty yards long. We cast anchor then, and I swam ashore with Bill and the Portugee, and the half-wit sat on the deck singing his song. All that the drunken man had said was more than true. I hardly like to call him drunken, when I think what he did for me, all out of pure kindness. But you know what I mean; he had had a few drinks and they had made him quick to notice things and quick to feel for other people, and perfectly truthful; you know the old proverb. Probably too the drinks had brightened his memory, even to tiny details like latitude and longitude. I shall never forget the peculiar crunch as we walked. The pearls were mostly the size of good large peas, and seemed to go down to about six or eight inches on to a hard grey sand; but to that depth of six or eight inches along that fifty yards, and from the sea to the cliff, the beach was entirely composed of them. From sea to cliff was about fifteen yards, so that if you multiply that by fifty yards for the length, and by half a foot for the depth, you will see how much that was of solid pearls. I haven't done the sum myself. They didn't go out under the sea; it was nothing but dead oyster shells there. A funny little current scooped around that bay; we could see it doing it still, though the shells were all empty now; but once it must have idly gathered those pearls, and idly flung them on to the little beach, and roamed away into the Indian Ocean beyond the gaze of man. Well, of course there was nothing to do but to fill our pockets, and we set about doing that; and it was a very curious thing—you may hardly believe me—but it was all I could do to get Bill to fill more than one pocket. Of course we had to swim back to the ship, which makes a reasonable explanation, but it wasn't Bill's reason at all. It was simply a fear he had of growing too rich. 'What's it worth?' he kept saying of his one pocketful. 'Over two hundred thousand,' I said at a guess. 'Can't see the difference between two hundred thousand and four hundred thousand,' Bill would say.

"'There's a lot of difference,' I'd tell him.

"'Yes, when I've spent the two hundred thousand,' Bill would go on.

"'Well, there you are,' I'd say.

"'And when will that be?' Bill would answer.

"I saw his point.

"And another thing he was very keen on. Bill seemed to have read of men who had come by big fortunes; won lotteries and one thing and another; and according to Bill they went all to pieces quickly, and Bill was frightened. It was all I could do to get him to fill the other pocket. The Portugee was quietly filling his, but with an uneasy ear taking in all Bill's warnings. You know there was something a bit frightening about all that wealth. There was enough of it to have financed a war, or to have ruined a good-sized country in almost any other way. I didn't stay more than a few minutes after my pockets were full, to sit on the beach and let the pearls run through my fingers. Then we swam back to the ship. I said to Bill, 'What about one more load of pearls?' For it seemed a pity not to. And Bill said only, 'Up anchor.' And the Portugee said, 'I expect that's best.' And the half-wit stopped his song and got up the anchor, and we turned homeward towards Aden.

"In little more than a fortnight we came to that cindery harbour, safe with our pearls. And there we sold a few in a quiet way, without waking suspicion, and paid the half-wit a thousand pounds for his wages, and went on to Port Said. The three of us took cabins on a large ship bound for London, in order to sell our pearls, and late one evening we came into Port Said and were to sail on next morning. By the time we'd paid off the half-wit and paid for our cabins we hadn't much ready money left, but Bill said he knew how to get some. Bill had gone pretty slow on drinks since he got the pearls, but gambling was a thing he would never give up. 'We can afford it now,' he used to say, which is of course what you never can do. So we went ashore at Port Said, and took our pearls with us, as we'd none of us trust all that out of our sight. And we came to a house Bill knew. Now, wasn't it a curious thing that Bill, who wouldn't trouble to put another two hundred thousand pounds in his pocket, was keen as mustard to make a hundred pounds or so in a Port Said gambling den? And it wasn't that he'd altered his mind about his pocketfuls of pearls being enough: he was never going back to that bay. Again and again I suggested it, but there was some sort of terror about that little white beach of pearls that seemed to have somehow got hold of him; or else it was some sort of general principle, perhaps inherited from simple folk for numberless generations, that seemed to warn him there was something unnatural and dangerous about so vast a display of easy wealth as lay on that beach in clear sunlight. I often wondered what it exactly was, that terror of the lovely little beach. It never quite caught me; unless at moments, at the turn of a thought, there may have seemed to be something lurking; but whatever it was it must have been lasting and strong to have kept that man in London leaning against a wall, and making no effort; nor ever likely to, as I judge, to go East into sunlight, and help himself to that wealth that in a generous drunken moment the good fellow had given to me.

"I wasn't keen on the gambling myself, but it seemed only friendly to keep an eye on the other two. So I slipped a revolver into my pocket and came with them. And I was probably drawn too by that feeling one used to have that, if the name of Port Said should turn up in a conversation, one has seen all that there is to see there. One liked to be able to say, if any particular den was mentioned, 'Oh yes, I dropped fifty pounds there.'

"I dropped more than that.

"Any way we came to the house; and Bill and I and the Portugee went in; and soon we were playing and winning. The stakes aren't high downstairs, and you usually win there. In fact that downstairs room reminded me of a trail of grain over grass leading up to a trap. Upstairs the stakes were much higher, and upstairs we asked to go. A Greek ran the show downstairs, the sort of Greek you might meet at night in the shadier parts of Port Said, and very often did: the man upstairs was a Greek too, but not the kind that you would count on meeting; he seemed worse than what I'd been warned against. As we walked in he looked at us, each in turn, and it was when he looked at you that his eyes seemed to light up, and the blood seemed to pale in his face, and all the man's power and energy went to those eyes.

"'High stakes here,' he said.

"I nodded my head, and Bill and the Portugee began to babble something.

"'Got the stuff?' snapped the Greek.

"The man's style irritated me. I suppose I lost my temper. Certainly Bill and the Portugee looked pretty angry at the way he was speaking to us. I never answered a word to him. I merely slipped a hand into my pocket and brought out a handful of pearls, all gleaming in the ugly light of that room. And the Greek looked at them with his lips slowly widening, for a long while before he spoke. And then he said, 'Pearls,' in quite a funny small voice. And I was just going to say Yes. It was like a page in a book, like a page with a picture of a man in a dingy room with pearls in his hand, just going to speak; you turn the page and come on something quite different, nothing to do with pearls, no room, and nobody speaking. Just silence and open air. And then the voice of a man coming up out of deeps of silence, saying the same thing over again, but with words that didn't as yet bring any meaning. A long time passed like that. Then the words again, and this time they seemed to mean something, if only one steadied oneself and tried to think.

"'He fainted in the street,' a man was saying.

"I was in a street right enough: I could see that as soon as I looked. And a man I had never seen before was saying that to a policeman. Fainted indeed! There was a lump on my forehead the size of two eggs, not to mention a taste in my mouth that I always get after chloroform."

"And the pearls?" blurted out the broker.

"The pearls," said Jorkens, and a sad smile shone for a moment. "Men found unconscious at night in the streets of Port Said never have pearls on them."

Jorkens remained shaking his head for a long time. "I suppose not," said someone to break the silence and bring him back to his tale.

"No," said Jorkens.

And after a while, in a voice that seemed low with mourning for his few weeks of fabulous wealth, Jorkens gave us what was left of his tale. "I never saw Bill or the Portugee again. Living or dead I never found trace of them. I took the policeman back to the house of the Greek, and was easily able to identify it. The downstairs room was the same as ever and I identified the man who ran it, as soon as we were able to wake him up and get him to come out of bed. What I couldn't do was to find the upstairs room, or even the staircase that led to it. As far as I could see we went all over the house, and I could neither say what had happened nor where it had happened, while the Greek was swearing by all kinds of things, that to him and the policeman were holy, that nothing had happened at all. How they'd made the change I was never able to see. So I just withdrew my charges, and gave the policeman backsheesh, and got back to the ship, and never saw any of my pearls again, except one that got lost in the lining, or ever saw trace again of the upstairs Greek. I got that one pearl in the lining fitted on to my tie-pin. Carrappas or Carrapaccas I could not find on any map, and no one I questioned in twenty sea-ports had ever heard of either; so, that one pearl back in my tie-pin was all I got out of the kindly advice of the drunken man by the wall."

"But the latitude and the longitude," said Terbut, with the quiet air of one playing a mate.

"You see, that," said Jorkens, "was what I couldn't remember."

The Walk to Lingham

"There's a kind of idea that I can't tell a story," said Jorkens, "without some kind of a drink. How such ideas get about I haven't the faintest notion. A story crossed my mind only this afternoon, if you call an actual experience a story. It's a little bit out of the way, and if you'd care to hear it I'll tell it you. But I can assure you that a drink is absolutely unnecessary."

"Oh, I know," I said.

"All I ask," said Jorkens, "is that if you pass it on, you'll tell it in such a way that people will believe you. There have been people, I don't say many, but there have been people that treated those tales I told you as pure fabrication. One man even compared me to Munchausen, compared me favourably I admit, but still he made the comparison. Painful to me, and painful, I should think, to your publisher. It's the way you told those tales; they were true enough every one of them; but it was the way you told them, that somehow started those doubts. You'll be more careful in future, won't you?"

"Yes," I said, "I'll make a note of it."

And with that he started the story.

"Yes, it's distinctly out of the way. Distinctly. But I imagine you will not disbelieve it on that account. Otherwise everyone that ever told a story of any experience he'd had would have to select the dullest and most ordinary, so as to be believed; an account of a railway journey, we'll say, from Penge to Victoria station. We've not come to that, I trust."

"No, no," I said.

"Very well," said Jorkens.

A couple of other members sat down near us then, and Jorkens said: "I can remember as if it was yesterday a long road in the East of England, with a border of poplars. It must have been three miles long, and poplars standing along it all the way on both sides of the road; right across flat fen-country. They had drained the fens, but patches of marsh remained, and here and all along ditches the pennons of the rushes were waving, like an army that had warred with ill success against man, scattered but not annihilated. And they hadn't contented themselves with draining the fens, for they had begun to cut down the poplars. That was what they were at when I first saw the road, with its two straight rows of poplars over the plain like green and silvery plumes, and I must say they were felling them very neatly. They were bringing them down across the road, as it was easier that way to get them on to the carts, and the amount of traffic they interfered with wasn't worth bothering over: in any case they could see it coming for three miles each way, if any ever came, and I never saw any, except the thing that I'll tell you about. Well, they were cutting one down that had to fall between two others across the road without making a mess of their branches, and there was only just room to do it with not two feet to spare. And they did it so neatly that it never touched a leaf: it came down with a huge sigh between the two other trees, and all the little leaves that were turned towards it waved and fluttered anxiously as it went past them with that great last breath. It was done so neatly that I took off my hat and cheered. Anyone might have done so. One doesn't set out to rejoice over those that are down, at least not openly. But one does not always stop to think, and it was perhaps five minutes before I began to be ashamed of that cry of triumph of mine echoing down the doomed avenue.

"It was the last tree they felled that day, and soon I was walking back alone to the village of Lingham where stood the nearest human habitations, three miles away over the fenland. And the glimmers of evening began to mellow the poplars. The woodmen with their carts and their fallen trees went the other way; their loud clear voices in talk, and their calls to their horses, soon fading out of all hearing. And then I was in a silence all unbroken but for my own footfall, and but for the faintest sound that seemed sometimes to murmur behind me, that I took for the sound of the wind in the tops of the poplars, though there was no wind blowing.

"I hadn't gone a mile when I had a sense, based on no clue, yet a deeply intense feeling, growing stronger and stronger for the last ten minutes, growing up from a mere suspicion to sheer intuitive certainty, that I was being furtively followed. I looked round and saw nothing. Or rather, partly obscured by a slight curve of the road I must have seen what I afterwards saw too clearly, and yet never credited what was happening. After that the more my sense of being followed increased, the less I dared look round. And none of the kinds of men that I tried to imagine as being what was after me seemed quite to fit my fears. I hadn't gone another quarter mile; I'd barely done another four hundred yards, when· but look here, I'm damned dry. I never had another experience like it, and looking back on it even today has parched my throat till I can hardly speak. I doubt if any of you have ever known anything of the kind."

"I'm sure we haven't," I said, and signed to the waiter, for there was no doubt that there was something in Jorkens' memory that could shake him even now. When he was quite himself again the first thing he did was to thank me, like the good old fellow he is, and then he went on with his tale.

"I hadn't gone another four hundred yards, when it was clear to me with some awful certainty that whatever was after me was nothing human. The shock of that was perhaps worse than the first knowledge that I was followed. There was no longer the very faintest doubt of pursuit; I could hear the measured steps. But they were not human. And, you know, looking over the fields all empty of men, level and low and marshy, I got the feeling, one got it very easily all alone as I was, that if there was anything there that had something against man, I was the one on whom its anger must fall. And the more that the fading illumination of evening made all things dim and mysterious the more that feeling got hold of me. I think I may say that I bore up fairly well, going resolutely on with those steps getting louder behind me. Only I daren't look round. I was afraid when I knew I was followed; I freely admit it; I was more afraid when I knew it was nothing human, yet I held on with a certain determination not to give way to my fears, except that one about not looking round. It wasn't the memory of anything I've told you yet that made my throat go dry just now." Jorkens stopped and took another long drink: in fact he emptied his tumbler.

"A frightful terror was still in store for me, a blasting fear that so shook me then that I nearly dropped on the road, and that sometimes even now comes shivering back on me, and often haunts my nights. We, you know, we are all so proud of the animal kingdom, and so absolutely preoccupied with it, that any attack from outside leaves us staggered and gasping. It was so with me now, when I learned that whatever was after me was certainly nothing animal. I heard the clod clod of the steps, and a certain prolonged swish, but never a sound of breathing. It was fully time to look round, and yet I daren't. The hard heavy steps had nothing of the softness of flesh. Paws they were not, nor even hooves. And they were so near now that there must have been sounds of large breathing, had it been anything animal. And at such moments there are spiritual wisdoms that guide us, intuitions, inner feelings; call them what you will. They told me clearly that this was none of us. Nothing soft and mortal. Nor was it. Nor was it.

"Those moments of making up my mind to look round, while I walked on at the same steady pace, were the most frightful in my life. I could not turn my head. And then I stopped and turned completely round. I don't know why I did it that way. There was perhaps a certain boldness in the movement that gave me some mastery over myself which just saved me from panic, and that would have of course been the end of me. Had I run I must have been done for. I spun right round and back again, and saw what was after me.

"I told you how I had cheered when the poplar fell. I was standing right under its neighbour. And men had been cutting down poplars for weeks. I remembered the look of that tree by which I had stood and cheered; chanced to note the hang of its branches. And I recognized it now. It was right in the middle of the road. One root was lifted up, with clods of earth clinging to it, and it was stumping after me down the road to Lingham. Don't think from any calmness I have as I tell you this that I was calm then. To say that I wasn't utterly racked with terror, would be merely to tell you a lie. One thing alone my reeling mind remained master of, and that was that one must not run. Old tales came back to me of men that were followed by lions, and my mind was able to hold them, and to act as they had taught. Never run. It was the last piece of wisdom left to my poor wits.

"Of course I tried to quicken my pace unnoticed. Whether I succeeded or not I do not know: the tree was terribly close. I turned round no more, but I knew what it looked like from the sound of its awful steps, coming up crab-like and elephantine and stumping grimly down, and I knew from the sigh in the leaves that the twigs were all bending back as it hurried after me. And I never ran.

"And the others seemed to be watching me. There was not that air of aloofness that inanimate things, if they really be inanimate, should have towards us; far less was there the respect that is due to man. I was terribly alone amongst the anger of all those poplars; and, mind you, I'd never cut one of them.

"My knees weren't too weak to have run: I could have done it: it was only my good sense that held me back, the last steady sense that was left to me. I knew that if I ran I should be helpless before the huge pursuit of the tree. It stands to reason, looking at it reasonably, as one can sitting here, that anything that is after you, whatever it is, is not going to let you get right away from it, and the more you try to escape the more you must excite it. And then there were the others: I didn't know what they would do. They were merely watchful as yet, but I was so frightfully alone there, with nothing human in sight, that it was best to go calmly on as though nothing was wrong, and making the most of that arrogance, as I suppose one must call it, that marks our attitude towards all inanimate things. As evening darkened the snipe began to drum, over the empty waste that lay flat and lonely all round me. And I might have felt some companionship, in my awful predicament, from these little voices of the animal kingdom, only that somehow or other I could not feel so certain as to what side they'd be on. And it is a very uneasy sound, the drumming of snipe, when you cannot be sure that it is friendly: the whole air moans with it. Certainly nothing in the sound decreased the pursuit of the tree, as one might have hoped it would, had any allies of the animal kingdom been gathering to befriend me. Rooks moved over, utterly unconcerned, and still the pursuit continued. I began to forget, in my terror, that I was a man. I remembered only that I was animal. I had some foolish hope that, as the rooks went over and the snipe's feathers cut through the air, these awful watchful poplars and the terror that came behind me might drop back to their proper station. Yet the sound of the snipe seemed only to add to the loneliness, and the rooks seemed only to aid the gathering darkness, and nothing turned the poplar as yet from its terrible usurpation. I was left to my miserable subterfuges; walking with a limp as though tired, and yet making a longer or quicker step with one leg than the other. Sometimes longer, sometimes quicker; varying it; and seeing which deceived the best. But these poor antics are not much good; for whatever is quietly following you is likely to judge your pace by the space between it and its prey, as much as by watching your gait, and to match its own accordingly. So, though I did increase my lead now and then, there soon grew louder again the swish of the air in the branches, and that clod clod that I hear at nights even now, whenever my dreams are troubled, a sound to be instantly recognized from any other whatever.

"Three miles doesn't sound far: it's no more than from here to Kensington: but I knew a man who was followed for far less by only a lion, and he swore it was longer than any walk he had ever walked before, or any ten. And only a lion, with breath and blood like himself; death perhaps, yet a death such as comes to thousands; but here was I with a terror from outside human experience, a thing against which no man had ever had to steel himself, a thing that I never knew I should one day have to face. And still I did not run.

"A change at last seemed coming over the loneliness. It wasn't merely the lights that began to shine from Lingham, nor the smoke from chimneys, the banner of man in the air; nor any warmth from the houses that could beat out as far as this: it was a certain feeling wider than warmth could go, a certain glow that one felt from the presence of man. And it was not only I that felt it: the poplars along the road were no longer watching me with quite that excited interest with which a while ago they had seemed to expect my slaughter."

"How did they show it?" said Terbut who can never leave Jorkens alone.

"If you had studied poplars for years and years," said Jorkens, "or if you had watched them as I watched them on that walk, when vast stretches of time seem condensed in one dreadful experience, you too would have been able to tell when poplars were watching you. I have seldom seen it since, and never again so as to be quite certain, but it was unmistakable then, a certain strained tensity in every leaf, twigs like the fingers of a spectre saying Hush to a village; you could not mistake it. But now the leaves were moving again in the soft evening air, the twigs seemed to be menacing nothing, and nothing about the trees was pointing or hinting or waiting; if you can use so mild a word as 'waiting' for their dreadfully strained expectancy. And better than all that, I had a hope—I could not yet call it any more—that my frightful pursuer was slowly dropping behind. And as I neared the windows the hope grew. Their mellow light, some reflecting the evening, some shining from lamps already, seemed throwing far over the marshes the influence of man. I heard a dog bark then, and, immediately after, the healthy clip clap clop of a good cart-horse, going home to his byre. The influence of these sounds on all nature can scarcely be estimated. I knew at once that there had been no revolution. I knew the animal kingdom was still supreme. I heard now unmistakably a certain hesitance come in the frightful footsteps behind me. And still I plodded on with my regular steps, whatever my pulse was doing. And now I began to hear the sound of geese and ducks, more cart-horses and now and then a boy shouting at them, and dogs joining in, and I knew I was back again within the lines of the animal kingdom; and had it not been for that terrible clod clod clod that I still heard behind me though fainter, I could have almost brought myself to disbelieve in the tree. Yes, as easily as you can, Terbut," for Jorkens saw he was about to say something, "sitting safely here." And in the end Terbut said nothing.

"When at last I reached the village the steps were far fainter, and yet I was still pursued, and only my fears could guess how far the revengeful tree would dare to penetrate into Lingham to face the arrogant mastery, and even the incredulity, of our kind. I hurried on, still without running, till I came to an inn with a good stout door. For a moment I stood and looked at it, door, roof and front wall, to satisfy myself that it could not easily be battered in, and when I saw it was really the shelter I sought, I slipped in like a rabbit.

"The brave appearance I kept up in front of the poplar dropped from me like a falling cloak, as I sat or lay on a wooden chair by a table, part of me on the table and part on the chair; till people came up and began to speak to me. But I couldn't speak. Three or four working men, in there for their glass of beer, and the landlord of the Mug of Ale, all came round me. I couldn't speak at all.

"They were very good to me. And when I found that the words would come again I said I had had an attack. I didn't say of what, as I might have blundered on to something that whiskey was bad for, and my life depended on a drink. And they gave me one. I will indeed say that for them. They gave me a tumbler of neat whiskey. I just drank it. And they gave me another. Do you know, the two glasses had no effect on me whatever. Not the very slightest. I wanted another, but before I took that there was one thing I had to be sure of. Was there anything waiting for me outside? I daren't ask straight out.

"'A nice village,' I said, lifting up my head from the table. 'Nice tree outside.'

"'No tree out there,' said one of the men.

"'No tree?' I said. 'I'll bet you five shillings there is.'

"'No,' he said, and stuck to it. He didn't even want to bet.

"'I thought I noticed something like a:' I daren't even say the word poplar, so I said 'a tree' instead. 'Just outside the door,' I added.

"'No, no tree,' he repeated.

"'I'll bet you ten shillings,' I said.

"He took that.

"'Well, go and have a look, governor,' he said.

"You don't think I was going outside that door again. So I said, 'No, you shall decide. I mayn't trust your memory against mine, but if you go outside and look, and say whether it's there or not, that's quite good enough for me.'

"He smiled and thought me a bit dotty. Oh Lord, what would he have thought me if I'd told him the bare truth.

"Well, he came back with the news that thrilled all through me, the golden glorious news that I'd lost my ten shillings. And at that I paid my bet and had my third tumbler of whiskey, which I did not dare to risk while I didn't know how things were. And that third whiskey won. It beat my misery, it beat my fatigue and my terror, and the awful suspicion which partly haunted my reason, that this unquestioned dominion that animal life believes itself to have established was possibly overthrown. It beat everything, and I dropped into a deep sleep there at the table.

"I woke next day at noon immensely refreshed, where the good fellows had laid me upstairs on a bed. I looked out over ruddy tiles; there was a yard below, with poultry, among walls of red brick, and a goat was tied up there, and a woman went out to feed him; and from beyond came all the ancient sounds of the farm, against which time can do nothing. I revelled in all these sounds of animal mastery, and felt a safety there in the light of that bright morning that somehow told me my dreadful experience was over.

"Of course you may say it was all a dream; but one doesn't remember a dream all those years like that. No, that frightful poplar had something against man, and with cause enough I'll admit.

"What it would have done if I'd run doesn't bear thinking of."

And Jorkens didn't think of it; with a cheery wave of his hand he made the sign to the waiter, that drowns memory.

The Escape from the Valley

When I arrived at the club they were all talking of earthquakes, those sudden dooms that so strangely overthrow cities, one shudder of Earth and the work of ages is over. But it was not of the ruin of whole towns that they told; one man had never seen that; they rather told of changes in little rooms, of Chaos running in suddenly upon respectable neatness, of gentility or domesticity or tawdriness coming suddenly cheek by jowl with the ancient powers, till the leaves of the aspidistras shivered with forces that had also rocked the hills. They were telling of curtain-rods gone wildly awry, of pictures swinging sideways, of the work of the housemaid and the dreams of the architect going down to the dust together. And suddenly at the end of a tale of a rocking city, somebody said, "You wait till Jorkens comes in, and you'll hear of worse earthquakes than any you ever saw." And this after a tale of an earthquake that had ruined a people, without any effort on their part.

I didn't think this entirely fair to Jorkens, and I don't now. What made it a great deal worse was that I knew that Jorkens was then on the stairs. We had arrived at the Club together, but he takes a bit longer over the stairs than I do. And before I had time to make any effective protest Jorkens was in the room. He made himself comfortable in the armchair he prefers, and at first he did little but breathe; but when we saw that this no longer presented any considerable difficulty to him, Terbut broke in with his question, for though it was someone else that made the first remark about Jorkens, Terbut is not the man to let a thing like that drop, while there is any chance of proving some theory he has about Jorkens's veracity. Exactly what the theory is I don't know, beyond that it is unjust to Jorkens, arising, as I suppose, out of some unaccountable jealousy, Terbut never having travelled much beyond Paris.

"We were talking of earthquakes," he said. "Have you ever been in one, Jorkens?"

"Well, yes," said Jorkens, "yes, I've been in an earthquake."

And we all bent forward to watch the duel between him and Terbut, a duel that was distinctly unfair, as Jorkens had no reason to guess that his word would be doubted, and that the more tremendous his earthquake the greater the triumph of Terbut, as it might appear to hasty or biasedopinion.

"Yes, I've been in an earthquake," said Jorkens. "The ground gave a kind of a shiver that you could not be sure of: a cart unloading near by, or a door slamming, might have done it, or a tree falling fifty yards away: I had the idea at once that it might be an earthquake, but until I saw a tile roll down a red cottage-roof and fall on the grass beside me I could not be certain. And then a cleft in a cliff far off, sheer smooth black rocks no more than a yard apart, came softly together like this." And Jorkens lifted his two hands, pointing upwards before his face, about an inch from each other, and moved them gently inwards until they touched.

"That was all," said Jorkens.

Was it possible that Jorkens had heard what was said as he came up the stairs, and had so triumphantly vindicated himself? Or had he all unconscious of any trap walked thus simply and grandly by it, stepping upon it and crushing it as he went? In any case he was vindicated.

"Well," said Terbut, with the air of one regretting the loss of the one tale he could have believed, "you never told us that story."

"No," said Jorkens, "it was an experience so terrible that I haven't liked to talk of it."

And Terbut for once seemed left without any comment.

"You see," said Jorkens, beginning slowly, but warming to it as he went on, "we were in a circular valley, obviously the crater of some ancient volcano, but extinct before ever man appeared on the planet. A little field and a lake, or pond, about the same size as the field, a cottage and a potato patch, were about all there were on the level base of the valley, from which green slopes led steeply up to the cliffs which were sheer all round, of black basalt. At their lowest point the cliffs were a hundred feet, and a pass led through them from the top of the green slope to another slope outside. But I'll tell you how it was that I came to be there. The Mediterranean is full of islands; and I got to know some of them pretty well; and of course they got to know me. Well, when I got into a certain amount of trouble one day over a girl, they all started saying: 'It's Yorkens again,' pronouncing it with a Y, like that. You know how talk spreads. And of course it had to be exaggerated a bit by every teller. Well, I thought the best thing to do was to go to some other island, one that would be out of the way of all that talk, for I was getting tired of it. So away I went, and I got to an island that seemed just the thing. But one evening as I was walking round the coast I saw this queer steep hill rising up from the sea something like half a mile away, and I asked some fishermen, drying their nets on the beach, to tell me something about it. And they said nobody went there, which wasn't true, because I saw a small boat with a sail drawn up on its beach, and true or not I wanted to go there: not much idle chatter, I thought, on an island that only ran to one small boat. Not that I had anything to be afraid of from anyone's chatter, but you know what girls are and the trouble they're apt to make. Very well. So I gave a fisherman one of their absurd silver coins, and he rowed me across to the island. There was no mistaking the way, a rough path led up from the beach through stunted ilex and myrtle on a slope that rose to perhaps five hundred feet, and there the black cliffs began and the sheer pass through them. You walked a hundred yards or so through the pass, and you came to the top of the green slope going down. Below me I saw the cottage of which I told you, with the red tiles of its roof, and the green field and the potato patch and the lake. It was all there was to see. The green slope went all round it perfectly circular, and the black cliffs rose above that, all the way round.

Now, you'll hardly believe it, but down in that cottage a man lived all alone with his sister. And that sister was remarkably pretty. He went once a week to the main island to get provisions; and she never saw anybody. There he lived quite content.

"I went down to that cottage and explained I was a travelling stranger, in as much of their language as I knew. And the man behaved perfectly sanely. But living there like that, a young fellow of under thirty, he might talk to me as politely as ever he pleased, but the first word I said to myself as soon as I gathered the situation, my very first word, was 'Crazy.' And I'd have gone away pretty quick, for I don't like craziness. Only that girl, as I told you, was pretty. What can one do when one's twenty-five or so, and comes on a pretty girl, a really very pretty one? It used to make me feel quite queer all over. I couldn't have gone away; I really couldn't even if I'd tried. So there I was, you see. I should never have hung about their house and trespassed on their hospitality and slept in their barn and dropped in again and again for meals, only for that. The last thing I ever expected there was a pretty girl: I wasn't looking for them, on the contrary I was rather running away from them. But there it was. Well, I hung about till I could see that the man could stand me no longer, and then I should have gone. That is certainly what I should have done; I see that. And I did say so to the girl, but she sighed so prettily when she said good-bye that I somehow unsaid it; I really hadn't the heart to say anything else.

"Next day he slipped off to the other island for food. If he'd spoken out like a man and told me to go, I suppose I should have, but he looked at me over his shoulder as he went, out of the corners of his eyes, a look so snake-like and slinking, that I should have done nothing for him after that unless he had asked for it on his knees, and even then I'd sooner have kicked him. Yes, he was my host, I know. But you never saw that look in his eyes. He had nasty teeth too. Very fine teeth, really; but the look of them was a nasty look. If you know what I mean.

"Well, he couldn't frighten me, though there was certainly something wrong about him, and you couldn't forget it. But the moment he was gone through the narrow pass I went straight and talked to the girl. She didn't mind. Well, what do you think? I was the only man she saw in a year. Unless you call that furtive brother a man.

"He wasn't gone an hour when the earthquake came. As I told you just now, I barely knew that it was one. I was standing by Liria, that was her lovely name, watching the black cliffs closing softly in on the pass, and I only saw them move because I was looking straight at the pass at the moment, for fear that the brother would come sneaking back, which was what neither of us wanted.

"I said to her that it looked to me like an earthquake, and then I turned to matters of greater interest and spoke again of herself. It was quite a while before I noticed that she was neither speaking nor listening to me, but was staring straight at the pass. It was closed, you see; and she was staring at it without blinking. Naturally the pass meant more to her than it did to me, she had known it all her life, and it took me some while to understand that there was really no other way out of the valley at all. When I did understand it I had a very uneasy time for two hours, which seemed a great deal longer. And it was getting dark, and the ducks were beginning to drop in to the lake, and I was wondering what on earth was going to happen, when that brother of hers appeared on the top in the falling light, and began letting a rope down. Of course we climbed up the slope to where the rope was, a hundred feet of it coming down over the cliff. And he began shouting 'Ladees first. Ladees first,' in an excited way from the top, as soon as she and I got hold of the rope. Of course I wasn't going first; the idea never entered my head; and I didn't need instruction in that sort of thing from a crazy foreigner. I helped her into the loop at the end of the rope and he began hauling her up. He seemed pretty strong and he got her up easily. And I sat down and waited for the rope to come back. I was pretty light in those days, barely nine stone, though you mightn't think it now; and I knew I should be no difficulty to him. I waited for him to take a rest after hauling up the girl: I was in no hurry. The rest seemed a very long one. The stars came out.

"I never thought what had happened, until I thought what that sort of man would do. And then I saw at once what he had done.

"Gone off and left me.

"Yes, he was that sort of fellow. And I might have known it by the look of his teeth.

"Well it was too late to bother now about what I might have foreseen, and if it hadn't been for that chance earthquake he'd have knifed me. I see that now. He'd probably gone to the main island to get a nice one, a good long knife with a curve on it. But slow starvation appealed to him more. It would. He was that sort of fellow. Probably lay awake calculating how I was getting on with the potatoes, which was all the food there was there, barring a day's provisions left in the cottage. It was the end of the week, and he'd gone over for fresh supplies. He'd know, that kind of fellow, to the last potato, how many I'd got, and how many days I could last on them. And he'd have been right, if I'd kept the potatoes to myself; but I didn't, I gave them to the ducks. Yes, ducks used to come to the lake in pretty large numbers, dropping in from the sea before nightfall, and going back again over the cliffs at dawn. Now a duck will always eat a potato, and I knew a way of catching them. The way to catch a wild-duck with a potato is to put a new potato on a plank stretched out over the water and fasten it by a string to a weight; and if you are barbarous enough you put a hook inside the potato. That was too cruel for me, so I arranged a noose instead, through which the duck had to put his neck in order to get at the food. Of course the hook is much simpler, but I wouldn't do it. You put your weight on the very edge of the plank, and as soon as the duck sees he is caught he tries to pull loose, and that upsets the weight, and down it goes with the duck under the water."

"Why have a weight at all?" said Terbut. "Why not tie the string to the plank?"

"Because," said Jorkens, "a fluttering duck in a trap scares all the others away. Not only that, but they never come back again. When your life depends on catching some ducks, you think of little things like that. And I didn't mean only to eat them; I had a scheme that may seem to you merely fantastic, as indeed it was, whereby they should carry notes for me asking for rescue. In the rush of thoughts that came when I saw I was trapped I evolved this scheme, and set a great deal of store by it; for one doesn't resign oneself all at once to the prospect of grubbing gradually through a potato-patch to die with the last potato. There was certainly no way over those cliffs, and of course I tried at the pass; but, do you know, you could hardly get in the blade of a knife there. If left to herself the girl would have sent me help; but she wouldn't be left to herself; I had no illusions on that point. So there I was in that miserable cottage with all my hopes pinned on a wild duck carrying a note. I wrote it out and arranged how to tie it; there was a whole ball of string in the cottage; and I finished up their provisions and made myself comfortable, and laid down the plank by the water to catch the duck; when suddenly the devastating thought occurred to me that these ducks would leave the lake at dawn and light on the sea, and that the only land they would come near would be my own desolate neighbourhood, to which they came every evening. The chance of a rare sportsman ever getting one of them was too remote for any serious plans; outside mere fiction there was no use for it. I was the only man that they ever came near, at the hour of the flight, after sunset, when they came in from the sea. And now it seemed a choice of living on the potatoes until they were finished, or living on ducks, which also must end as soon as the potatoes were over, for I had no other way of catching them. I knew well enough that that crazy brother would go off with Liria to some other small island, and that I should never see or hear of either of them any more. Well, I preferred ducks to potatoes, but I knew that it couldn't last; the flight itself doesn't last all the year round, let alone new potatoes, and it was getting late in the year; one of these days a thin film of ice would appear on the lake, and not a duck would come near it: I knew the ways of ducks; not that it took much knowledge to know that they wouldn't come to swim in a pond that was frozen over.

"In these desperate straits I had to think, and thinking was no good, and then there came to me suddenly a sheer inspiration; it was nothing less than that, and nothing less would have saved me. There was no way out of that valley, and without that sudden flash I'd have left my bones there. I'd been thinking over my plan to send a letter tied to a duck, and calculating that a duck could easily carry five or six ounces; and then the inspiration came flashing down out of nowhere, without any preparation on my part or any guess whatever that it was coming; and the inspiration was simply this, the little golden words that saved my life: If one duck can carry five ounces two ducks can carry ten. Never in all my life has so blessed an idea come to me. Water in a desert was nothing to it, nor home to the exile, nor food to the nearly starving: it was all these things to me, and life and liberty too. And it was sheer good practical truth. I mean, after all, twice two is four."

"We know that," said Terbut.

"Well," said Jorkens, "and two hundred times two is four hundred. It was only a matter of getting enough ducks. I told you I was under nine stone in those days, and with enough ducks I could carry it, if only the new potatoes held out."

"Carry yourself?" exclaimed Terbut.

"The difficulty," said Jorkens, "was getting enough ducks.

"They were there in plenty and my new potatoes would catch them, but they had to be caught quick, or my food would give out and there would be nothing of me left to carry out of that valley. All I dare give them was just over five ounces each, three to a pound, forty-two to a stone, and three hundred and fifty to carry me: it was an awful lot of ducks. In fact it was too many, and I daren't give them any more weight. I luckily had the ball of string, and a good lot of potatoes. But I hadn't the time. Either I must eat potatoes and there wouldn't be enough for the ducks, or I must live on the ducks, and would never get enough of them at that rate. That was my difficulty. Well I calculated that without my boots and my coat and waistcoat I could get down to eight stone, and that would be three hundred and thirty-six ducks, giving them each a third of a pound, and I felt I daren't give them more. I don't know what a duck can carry, but that was just what I felt about it.

"Well I got my planks down to the water; I took the damned fellow's floor boards; and I laid out my new potatoes with bricks attached, and lay under covert, and the flight came in. And sure enough they went for my new potatoes. They came in almost straight, without any wheeling, by which I saw the sly brother never had had a gun; nor would he have had; he was no sportsman. But confident though they were, and pleased with my new potatoes, they were not going to stay there while I walked down to the water. That was the difficulty.

If I went for a duck to pull him out of the water the whole lot would go. And I couldn't last for a year, catching one a night; three weeks was more like it, at the outside.

"And yet I caught twelve of them the first night. I did it like this. A duck can live under the water an enormous long time: the very first thing that a winged duck does is to dive whenever he can get to water, and if he does reach it you seldom see him again. How long he can live without air I do not know; again I had to guess, as I had with the weights. But any way I was sure they could do five minutes, probably without any discomfort. So I waited five minutes after the first one was caught and then walked down to the water. In that time I had caught twelve.

"Somehow I hardly ever caught more than that. Many of them came back the same night, but I daren't catch any more and show myself a second time, or they might have left the lake altogether after being disturbed twice in one night.

"My days weren't idle: I had to house the ducks in boxes and any woodwork that I could put together, and I had to grub up potatoes to feed them and feed myself and to catch more in the evening. And the sun would set and the splendours fade from the sky; and, sure as starlight, the ducks would come dropping in.

"Sometimes I ate a duck, but mostly potatoes; but as the three weeks began to draw to a close, and I could never, or rarely, get more than a dozen each night, I began to see I should never be able to do it. At the end of twenty days I had two hundred and forty-three ducks, and I wanted three hundred and thirty-six. One more day and, by my calculations, my food was done unless I ate ducks, and if I did that I was further off than ever from getting the number in time. I felt I was done, and I was sorry; sorry to die, and sorry too that my plan had failed, for no one else so far as I knew had done it; a perfect plan with no flaw in it whatever, but Time was against me, and had won. Well, I made a desperate struggle, as much for the sake of my plan as anything. The twenty-first day was the last day I ate food, and I only caught ten ducks that day. After that I gave all the potatoes to the ducks in my coops, and for three days I ate nothing. I did well in those three days, catching forty-two, a little above the average: I had two hundred and ninety-five ducks, but I could do no more. I looked at my figures and felt that I was beaten. I couldn't last out without food for another day. But do you know what those three days had done? They had taken a stone off me. I suddenly realized that I couldn't be more than seven stone; two hundred and ninety-four ducks could do it, and I had one over. Not only that but on that last night I tried a second time and caught several more.

"I had the others all harnessed already, that is to say a piece of string looped round their bodies in front of their wings and again behind, and a length hanging down; and several tied together in bunches. And I had another round my waist. Perhaps these details may bore you."

"Not at all," said Terbut, hoping to catch him out.

"But," Jorkens went on, "I had to have some control on the various bunches of ducks, or they'd have all got entangled. You know what ducks are when they get frightened. But by moving a knee or an ankle I could regulate them a bit. I needn't tell you that ball of string wasn't enough, though it came in very handy. I tore that damned fellow's sheets and curtains to shreds, and didn't even stop at bits of my own clothing, before I had threads enough to get everything fixed up neatly.

"Well, I was naturally in a hurry to be off: I'd eaten nothing for three days. But all that took time. By about 3a.m. I was ready. And then I waited for dawn. It was a long time coming; I've noticed, knocking about the world as I've done, that dawn very often is. I don't quite know what's the cause of it."

"The rotation of the earth," said Terbut.

"I expect so," said Jorkens. "Well, I got two large bunches of them held down by passing the ends of the strings underneath a couple of rocks, and I had another rock tied round my waist. I had all the ducks fastened on except those two bunches which I meant to take in my hands. They made an infernal noise. The sky lit up suddenly from the other side of the cliffs. I cut the string that held the rock to my waist, grabbed the other strings, one bunch in each hand, and wrenched them free from the rocks, and we were off.

"I can tell you I was very glad to be leaving that valley. And that last night in the hunger and cold was the longest: winter was coming on and I had no coat or boots, and there are two other things that always make you cold, which perhaps you don't know, Terbut; one is hunger, and the other is want of sleep. I was pretty cold when I started, but that was nothing of what I felt going through the sharp morning air; and yet I didn't mind, for I was going towards freedom, and away from that slow death the sly brother of Liria had planned for me. Yes, we were going all right; back towards the sea along the very line that the ducks always flighted. But they were dragging a bit. I began to see there was something wrong with my figures. It began to be doubtful if we could clear the cliff. If we dropped back this time we were done: no more potatoes for the ducks, and I couldn't get any lighter than seven stone and live. The cliff drew nearer and nearer. The ducks were clear of it, but would I be? My feet actually brushed the top, but it was the top. I gave a kick to the ground and we soared six feet, and we were over and sloping downwards to the sea.

"The morning was glorious from the top of the cliffs; the whole sea shone with it. But I didn't want to go out to sea with those ducks. So as soon as we got near the beach I loosed the bunch I held in one hand. That brought us down with a bit of a bump, though not to the ground; but it taught me that it wouldn't be safe to let the other handful go while we were over anything hard. So I had to wait till we were over the sea. The ducks weren't pulling very well by then, and we certainly did come down pretty hard when I loosed the second handful. Of course the water broke the fall, but it wasn't very deep: I had to come down in the shallows so as to be able to deal with the ducks. I had to stand up and cut them loose one by one. Well, perhaps I've talked enough. I stood and waved on the beach, and I soon attracted a fisherman from the main island. And that was the end of that. But you can understand that, left for three weeks in such a position as that, with such a prospect before me, I don't talk of that bit of an earthquake merely for pleasure."

Jorkens ceased. It's usual at our Club, especially with Jorkens, if anyone entertains with a story, to offer him a whiskey and soda at the end. It's only our way of saying thank you. But on this occasion member after member, of those that had heard this tale, quietly ordered one for themselves. If any perplexities urged them to this slight stimulant, I too was perplexed. There were points that I could not, as it were, see before me; while different things that Jorkens had told us seemed to be at variance in my mind with contrary ideas of my own. Then I also signed to the waiter and had a whiskey. At once the apparent contradictions were clear, and, with a better grip of just what had happened, I could see that Jorkens's tale was perfectly true.

An August in the Red Sea

As I came into the Club the other day they were talking of elephants. Much more sagacious than dogs, they were saying. Well, it doesn't really matter what they were saying, as none of it was new, or even out of the ordinary. "But they remember an injury for ages," said another of them. "Revengeful beasts," said another. And gradually from then on, the elephant began to lose, so far as the Billiards Club was concerned, his reputation for intellect, in exchange for one of long and revengeful brooding. And that is how it would have been left but for Jorkens, and distinctly unfair to the elephant. But Jorkens broke in on a tale of long-brooded revenge over some trifling matter of a bad orange with the words: "That's nothing to men."

"Men?" we said surprised at such a comparison.

"Yes," said Jorkens. "Nothing to the way they'll brood and revenge themselves."

We didn't think humanity was as petty as all that. Why, to be human means the very opposite of all that sort of thing. And so we said. And Jorkens, to prove his point, said: "I knew a man once, a Greek, who thought he was laughed at or slighted. And he planned for two years to fool the man that had made a fool of him, and at the end of that time he did it, and it must have cost him thousands and thousands. What do you think of that? Would an elephant spend all that time and money over such a trifle? No, it takes a man to be such a damned fool as that."

"But what did he do?" we asked.

"I'll tell you," said Jorkens.

And that's how I came to hear that singular story of August in the Red Sea.

"This Greek," said Jorkens, "was on a British liner going southwards down the coast, travelling on business. He was a glass manufacturer somewhere in Egypt, and he got on at Port Sudan. I imagine he made pretty well all the tumblers and wine-glasses in Egypt, and he was making that journey so as to extend his business to Durban and Capetown. I was only going to Durban myself. Well, we came to the line, and this Greek had never crossed it before. We had the usual game crossing the line, and the ship's officers took it all up very keenly and helped to make the fun go. Of course we had Neptune on board, with a fine beard made out of rope, and, well of course the joke's not very funny, so they did all they could to make it go, trying to amuse the passengers to make them forget the heat, and of course some got ducked in a swimming bath, which helped to cool them too. It wasn't that that seems to have irritated the Greek, but being told by the captain that this really was Neptune, just come out of the sea. Of course the captain was only trying to make it go; so as to amuse everybody. An elephant would have seen that much. But this Greek felt himself insulted by being treated, as he called it, like a child, because—as he said—he was a foreigner. And of course that wasn't the reason at all, he was only selected because he had never crossed the line; it was his turn; and any fooling there was was only done to make the passengers forget the blistering heat. Anyhow he flared up. 'We gave Neptune to the world,' he said, 'before the rest of Europe was civilized. We, the Greeks. And they think they can treat me like a child. Me, a Greek. We fooled the world with Neptune, before you were civilized.'

"'Poseidon, wasn't it,' I said, to check his fury, for it was mounting higher and higher and I didn't know what he would do.

"'Yes,' he shouted with the most triumphant scorn, 'and you could never even get the name right.'

"Well, after that I said no more. It doesn't sound much of a score, but from the way he shouted it he seemed to think he had vindicated Greece against the whole of Europe, and I thought at first that that would have satisfied him, but not a bit of it, he went away and brooded; said no more for the rest of the voyage, and made his absurd and elaborate plans to be revenged on the captain by fooling him and his officers as they, as he put it, had tried to fool him.

"Well, I got off at Durban, and in two years' time I was on the same ship again. I used to knock about the East African coast a good deal in those days, going to one place and another. It is quite untrue that I ever poached ivory; I never had anything to do with it, as my detractors will find out if they ever dare put it in writing. I was on the same ship going northwards, and at the very end of August we entered the Red Sea. Well of course, you know, that can be a frightful experience. Two deserts lie like the sides of an oven, and the Red Sea is in between. They light the fires in March, and by the end of August these two deserts, that you can barely touch with the palm of your hand, have the Red Sea done to a turn, and it begins to cool in November. Men not in the least emotional start at a point, in heat like that, when very little more is required to drive them clean crazy. And it was a particularly bad August, even for the Red Sea.

"Well, I was sitting on the deck about lunch-time, and the rest of us were below having lunch. What on earth they wanted to have lunch for in that heat I can't imagine. I had the best kind of deck-chair."

"What kind is that?" Terbut interrupted quite needlessly.

"There are only two kinds," said Jorkens; "the one with a hole to hold a tumbler in one of the arms of the chair; and the other kind has two holes. I was lying in my deck-chair, when the captain came running up with a note in his hand that they'd evidently sent down from the bridge. He came out on the passengers' deck because it was the nearest deck to the dining saloon. We were just passing a rocky island. The captain went to the side and looked out ahead of the island. Then he put up his glasses, and when he took them down I distinctly saw tears in his eyes."

"Tears!" said Terbut.

"Yes," said Jorkens. "They were running down his face."

"Sweat," said Terbut.

"Sweat? Of course there was sweat," said Jorkens. "It was the Red Sea in August. But these were tears, and he went and sat down in one of the chairs and sobbed.

"I went to the side myself then and looked over, round the corner of that red island where the captain had looked; and about a mile from the island I saw what he had seen. I went straight to my cabin and lay down and kept quite quiet, and sent for the ship's doctor. I said: 'It's not my brain, doctor. It's my eyes. My brain's all right.'

"And he said: 'That's all right. I'll give you something for it.' And I said: 'Doctor, I'm not going to touch a drink all day. I'm going to do just what you tell me.'

"And he said: 'That's quite all right. I'll send you something by the steward, and don't get up till I see you again. It's very hot.'

"And I drank it when it came, and slept for twelve hours. And as soon as I woke I knew that everything was all right."

"Yes, yes," said Terbut, "but you tell us that you saw the captain of a British ship in tears?"

"It was the heat," said Jorkens. "I tell you it was at the end of August in the Red Sea, not thirty miles from the Gates of Hell, as they call them, and no straits are better named. It was that still, oven-like heat. And then suddenly seeing this, and thinking his reason had broken down, and his career ended; never another job for him at sea again; and a family, likely as not, brought to the brink of starvation, at any rate all their leisure and comforts gone. He'd never have given way like that in England, or on any decent sea; but the heat there is perfectly frightful; and seeing a thing like that all of a sudden, when he was limp with the blazing heat."

"But what was it?" we shouted, for he really seemed to be rushing past the point.

"Well, of course it must have been some fake of that damned glass-manufacturer," said Jorkens. "That Greek I told you of. He had no real competitors in the glass trade in the whole of that continent; so he could afford to do anything."

"Yes, yes, yes. But what was it?" asked Terbut.

"An ice-berg," said Jorkens.

"An ice-berg!" came from us all, quick as a cough.

"Yes," said Jorkens with an earnest sadness, "and what went to my heart in that frightful heat, and so far away from home, was a little patch of snow that it had on the top. Frosted glass, I dare say; but it went right to my heart."

The Bare Truth

An incident occurred the other day at the Club that I disliked very much. Perhaps incident is too strong a word for it; for after all it was trivial and passed unnoticed; yet it was one of those things that can do no good, and are always better avoided. Jorkens had just told a story: I do not repeat it here, since I wish only to offer my readers those stories of Jorkens that nobody can disprove, while in place of proofs that they are actually true I confidently rely instead on the sporting sense of the reader, which will not permit him to disbelieve Jorkens' word merely because positive proof is not to hand at the moment.

Jorkens then had told a tale, and there were points about it that caused me to reserve my judgment before giving it that unqualified belief that would entitle me to offer it to my reader, and we were about to discuss it amongst us and ask Jorkens a few questions, which would no doubt have made everything clear, when one of our members, whose name I will not give, said: "Jorkens, have you ever told the truth in your life?"

I admit that he said it with a smile, which certainly removes it from accusations and places it amongst jokes; yet even as a joke I did not like it, and without wishing to generalize I think it is often the case that remarks that need a smile to make them possible are really better unsaid. I will say no more in criticism of a member of the club to which I also belong. The rest is sheer praise. Jorkens was admirable. If I have exposed one slip at our club, I offer the behaviour of another member as a model. Who, being suddenly asked if he had ever spoken the truth in his life, would show the restraint Jorkens showed? How many members can any club boast who could so deftly answer such a question as this without any traces of rancour?

"Yes, once," Jorkens answered. "I wonder if any of you may have had the same experience? Once for the best part of an hour I told the most pure undiluted absolute truth. I'll tell you how it occurred. I was in a town called Dead Horse, in South Africa. It's out on the veldt, about thirty miles west of the railway. Corrugated iron mostly. I often thought the native quarter looked more comfortable. Well, I'd gone there to sell a mine for a man in the City. What city? There's only one, as far as I know. I'd gone there to sell a mine for him. The mine was at Dead Horse; a gold mine, you know. And I'd got the man there on the spot, that was to buy it. I'd got him at Dead Horse. He came from Kimberley. He was a fellow called Steig, I remember. And it wasn't one of these mines that you get a prospectus about, and invest your money, and that's all you see of the mine. No, this was a mine that was there, a mile out from Dead Horse, and I took Steig to see it.

"Well, I knew something about it of course, but, I must say, I was astonished when I saw it. I went over it with Steig and we both had a look at it. It was full of nuggets: Steig picked up at least a dozen, anything from five to ten ounces each, and there were rocks with lodes in them that fairly glittered. White quartz, you know, and all streaky with gold. Even I was surprised at it. Then we came back to Dead Horse to a thing that they called an hotel, to talk it over.

"The mine was to go for a million, and I was to have ten per cent of the price, whatever it was. I was allowed a certain latitude for haggling, but a million was the idea. And, you know, ten per cent on a million's a lot of money.

"Well, Steig offered me whiskeys, but I knew what he was after. You see, the man that owned this mine knew a lot about it. There are things known in the City that you don't pick up by poking round lumps of quartz for an hour, even if you do think you are the man on the spot. Steig knew that much, and he wanted to find out what they knew in the City about it. In vino veritas was his idea; and he fancied I knew, having come straight out from England. Well, the more he offered me whiskey the more I drank water, which is a damned dangerous drink out there. But it was my duty to keep my head, my duty to those that employed me; so I drank the stuff and chanced it, and kept away from the whiskey. And, as it turned out, it did me no harm.

"Well, towards the end of the evening Steig went to a cupboard, and rather quietly unlocked it and slipped a bottle out, and filled a liqueur-glass from it, half turning his back to me, and drank it off without ever saying a word. And very soon after that he went to bed.

"Next day we took another look at the mine, and Steig came away with more nuggets and had them tested; and after sunset we sat again in his room, in the thing they called an hotel, he drinking whiskeys and soda, and I drinking water and pretending to like it, holding it up to the light and looking at it approvingly, but in silence, because I didn't know how you praised water. And this time when he went to the cupboard and got the other bottle he put it on the table, but on the far side from me and made a point of not offering it me. Of course we were talking shop, part of the time openly, and part of the time we were talking of flowers and butterflies just to give the impression that the mine or the million didn't really mean much to us; but really, whether it was butterflies or flowers, we were talking shop all the time. One thing I couldn't help noticing about that other drink of his was that, while I was pretending to like water, he really did like his drink. I noticed it all the more because I was pretending myself. A look that I can only call ecstasy came over his face with each sip that he took from his liqueur-glass.

"Well, it wasn't only that I was sick of the water, but I began to be irritated at his ideas of how to do host. I even suggested to him that he appeared fond of that drink. But he pushed it further away, and said that he only drank it for his health. No more than that would he say. And, as for offering me any, I might as well have asked for the Southern Cross. I got so irritated that in the end I said I wouldn't sell him the mine; and, when he asked me why, I said that a mine like that for a million was an opportunity that didn't come everyone's way, and that, if he didn't care to give me what might be a rare drink, I wouldn't let him have what was certainly a rare mine, as he had seen with his own eyes. And I said that not everybody who was sold a mine was allowed to go all over it as he had done, before deciding to buy. For a while he tried to get out of giving up a drop of the drink, but all of a sudden he seemed to see that I wouldn't have that, for all at once he gave in and poured out half a tumbler, and refused to pour any more.

"I never knew what it was made of. I never knew. Nectarines and honey, I should say, to a great extent. But, oh, it was a wine. And there was a fire in it like processions of torches going through vineyards along the borders of Heaven. The sunlight in it seemed to be flaming still. Oh, it was a wine, a wine indeed. And as soon as I had drunk that half tumbler up I had no difficulty in asking Steig for some more, for I had an eloquence now that none could resist, a glory of splendid words that would have made bees give up their honey. Half of a minute of that speech and he had filled the tumbler again for me.

"I was not drunk. I have never been drunk in my life. I was in a reverie. I fell into a golden reverie. And in the reverie I heard my own voice prattling of memories so remote from there that they must have been the very earliest things that my mind had ever stored. I remembered a garden that I once had had, a garden one yard square. I remembered sowing wheat in it. I told, I heard my voice telling, of my delighted wonder, when I saw the tiny green blades really arising. They had said that wheat grew like this; but, when I saw it really growing, my delight was beyond bounds. I had forgotten it utterly, and now I heard my own voice reminding me of it again after all those years; and from childhood to twenty-five seems longer than any other stretch of years we know. I told of the difference between weeds and flowers, a knowledge so slowly come by, so hard to accept; for who could believe at first that that glowing light the dandelion, that proud exuberance of colour, was only a weed? My voice brought back to me many a tiny splendour that shone to brighten the shadows of English lanes, and I heard it telling over strange rustic cures for many a simple ailment, and blessing the dock-leaf for its help in time of need, whenever the lurking nettle had found bare knees, or too curious hands had rashly come on the nettle. Weeds all these, but weeds once loved. Then an awe came into my voice and it told of the splendour of may, gleaming out over acres of untended land, that no one tilled, no one troubled, and the scent of it so filling the sunny air that it seemed as if the world for miles was enchanted. It told of flowers coming proudly up, tall and bright in great gardens, gardens enlarged by the glitter and distance of childhood till they loomed as big as a mile-square garden might now. It was not memory that was inspiring my voice, for I made no effort to remember before I spoke: it was my voice that brought back memories, lost in immense distances; they came back again to me, borne on my own words, like the scent of lilac suddenly carried by winds. As I talked on, reliving my lost years, the memories grew more familiar, arising less surprisingly out of the dark of the past; they began to be memories that I knew that I treasured, yet they were no more true than the ones that I thought were lost.

"I told of my school-days, I told of my growing up, I told of my first love. More than I shall ever tell you I told Steig in that iron shed that they called an hotel. And my voice went babbling on.

"There came clear to my reverie the first job I ever got, and how that led to a better one, and that to a better one still, though nothing ever equalled my pride in the first. And then one day I got this job with the man in the City, who had the mine to sell. And he sent me all the way to South Africa with carte blanche. That, I think, was something for a young man to be proud of, to be sent from the City of London to sell a mine in South Africa for a million, and absolute trust in his discretion. It was something to be proud of indeed, and something I might well have boasted of, even if I had been strictly sober in the narrowest sense of the word. I have heard men boast of far less. And a good mine too. Salted of course. I mean the nuggets didn't get there all by themselves; but real nuggets, and plenty of them. Not worth a million of course, but what did you expect? Did he think that a financier in the City of London was going to send me all the way there to do a deal just for the benefit of Steig. Take it as he found it. It was worth a thousand or two with all those nuggets in it, even if the lodes in the quartz were gilded lead. Of the lodes I knew nothing, for my firm had never informed me; but I knew the nuggets were genuine, because I knew the men in the City who had supplied them, men straight as a die. And in any case Steig had tested them. That was the way to look at it; look at the actual value of the nuggets that he had found already; count on finding a good dozen more; and then see what he could get for it in the South African market, a mine well worth considering, business being what it is.

"Yes, I found my voice saying all that. I did indeed. And just as dreams are vividest before waking, I remembered that part of my reverie the most clearly, and I remember it word for word still. They say, Magna est veritas et prevalebit, meaning you can't shake off truth; and I wish I could; those words I heard my voice prattling brightly to Steig are echoing in my ears to this very day. And all of a sudden I came out of my reverie.

"And later, when I tried to get down to business, I found Steig in a sunny mood. He said that he was delighted to have met me, and hoped that we should often meet again, and that it wasn't often in a place like Dead Horse, or, as he was good enough to say, anywhere in South Africa, that he had the opportunity of meeting anybody like me. He really went on and on along those lines for so long that I tried to stop him, and when at last I did, and when I could get him to business, he said that he liked the mine very much and would have bought it, but that unfortunately an aunt of his whom he had expected to be sending a million had forgotten to send him any money at all, and that for this reason he would have to decide to do without the mine.

"Of course the nuggets were all thrown back, and the mine was as good as ever; but it had somehow got about, all over South Africa, that it was a mine that Steig didn't want. And the truth is; but I think we've had enough of truth for one day."

What Jorkens Has To Put Up With

To say that amongst all those that have read any of the tales of Mr. Jorkens' travels that I have recorded, none has felt any doubts of any of them would be absurd: such doubts have been felt and even expressed. But what has impressed me very considerably is the fair-minded attitude taken up by the general public, an attitude that may be summarized as a firm determination not to disbelieve a man's story merely because it is unusual, but to await the final verdict of science when science shall have arrived at the point at which it is able to pronounce on such matters with certainty. Then, should the verdict be against Jorkens, and not till then, will a sporting public turn upon him that scornful disbelief that they are far too fair-minded to show without good and sufficient proofs. I myself meanwhile am careful to record nothing he tells me, against which anyone in the Billiards Club or elsewhere has been able to bring any proof that would definitely rule it out in a court of law. And it would be interesting to see for how long in such a court arguments that may be lightly advanced now, against the exact truth of any one of his tales, would stand up against the ridicule of counsel. But the sporting attitude that the public have adopted towards him is more to Jorkens than a verdict in any court of law. Curiously enough it is in the Billiards Club itself, the source of all these stories, that the most unsporting attitude is often shown to Jorkens. For instance only the other day one of our members was unnecessarily rude to him, though with only a single word. I need hardly say it was Terbut. The word was not in itself a rude one, but was somehow all the more insidious for that. Also it was really a single word, and not a short sentence, as is often the case when a writer says to you "I will tell it to you in one word." But I will tell the story.

We were discussing billiards, which is not a thing we often do in the Billiards Club. There is, I suppose, some sort of feeling that, if anyone talks of billiards there, his imagination or his experience can provide him with nothing better; billiards being, as it were, bed-rock in the Billiards Club. In just the same way at the Athenaeum, although the bird is inseparable from the Club's presiding goddess, one seldom, if ever, orders an owl for one's lunch. But we were discussing billiards today, and debating whether bonzoline balls or the old ivory kind were the better. I will not record the discussion, for it has nothing to do with Jorkens, but it may interest my readers to hear that it was held at the Billiards Club that the bonzoline ball was unique among modern substitutes, in being better than the old genuine article. It was as we had decided that, that some young member who ought to have known better, seeing Jorkens near him as he looked up, suddenly blurted out: "Have you ever seen a unicorn, Jorkens?"

Of course it was not the way to speak to an elder man. Of course the implication was obvious. And Jorkens saw in a moment that the young fellow did not believe in the existence of unicorns at all. In any case he had not yet passed that time of life, in which one believes nothing that the ages have handed down to us until we have been able to test it for ourselves.

"I deprecate that hard and fast line between fabulous animals and those that you all chance to have seen," said Jorkens. "What does it amount to, practically, but a line drawn round Regent's Park? That's all it is really. Everything inside that line is an animal you readily believe in. Everything outside it is fabulous. It means you believe in an animal if you have seen it in the Zoo, otherwise not. However full history is of accounts of the unicorn, and the most detailed descriptions, still you go off to Regent's Park on a Sunday, and if there is not one there waiting for your bun you disbelieve in the unicorn. Oh well, I was like that myself till I saw one."

"You saw one?" said the young fellow who had started the topic.

"I'll tell you," said Jorkens.

"I was camped once by the Northern Guaso Nyero, or rather I was camped two hundred and fifty yards from it, a distance that just makes all the difference, for two hundred yards is all that the mosquito flies from his home. Of course he has a good many homes, that's the trouble; but, as he prefers a river frontage, it's a very good thing to camp that far from a river. Not that it amounts to much, for Africa can always get you some other way. But there it was. Well, I was collecting heads for a museum, and had been at it for some time, with a white hunter and eighty natives, trekking through Africa; and I was beginning to get pretty tired of it. I was sitting by one of our campfires after supper, with the white hunter beside me, and I was gazing into the glow of the smouldering logs and watching the fireflies gliding backwards and forwards, and thinking all the while of the lights of London. And the more the fireflies slowly grew into multitudes, and the more the fire glowed, the more I longed for London. In that mood I asked the hunter what we should do next day; and, whatever he suggested going after, I pointed out I had shot it already. Which was perfectly true.

"And winds came out of the forest, or over the plains, and softly played with the smoke going up from our logs of cedar, and the visions changed and changed in the glow of the fire, and every now and then the hunter would make some new suggestion, till I said petulantly: 'Find me something I haven't shot yet.'

"And he said: 'Very well, I will.'

"'What is it?' I said.

"And he wouldn't say.

"I kept on asking him, but he wouldn't tell me. The man whose job it was, the askari we called him, came and put more logs on the fire, and we sat on long with little cold winds on our backs and the warmth on our hands and feet, but still he would not say. 'Why not?' I asked him at last. 'Because you'd think me mad,' he said. 'Well, aren't you?' I asked. Partly my insinuation was true, and partly it was the product of some unreasonable irritation that had come over me, and Africa was responsible for both.

"Next day he moved our camp to the edge of the river, and we waited there a long time; I don't remember how long, quite a fortnight; and all the while he stuck to his promise to find me this new beast that I had never shot.

"I began to get malaria, and so did he. And then one night as we were talking of remedies, for we were both tired of quinine, he told me what it was we were looking for. Yes, simply a unicorn. He had had natives out in the forest searching for it for weeks, and though they had not yet seen it they had at last found the spoor. And then he explained to me about how to get a unicorn. The animal, he explained to me, was always fairly cautious of men, and on the whole, in spite of exceptions, had tended to avoid them more than do other animals; but that of late centuries, probably since the invention of fire-arms, or since some other change in the ways of men, it had avoided men so assiduously that it had almost dropped out of history. Up to the time that a Pope gave the horn of one to King François one day in the fifteenth century, and for a while after, references to the unicorn are so frequent that its avoidance of man, however much wished by the unicorn, can only be called unsuccessful; after that time a cunning unknown before seems to have been added to its love of elusiveness, with the result that it is no longer classed among European mammals.

And then the hunter explained to me how to get one. There was no way whatever to come at him, he explained, except one, and that was to drive him. And then he drew out some paper and a bit of pencil, and showed me how it was done: he made a row of dots in a semi-circle to represent beaters, and put a cross in the middle to mark the unicorn, and showed me how the flanks came gradually in. His hand was rather shaky with malaria, and I couldn't see very well either, but the thing seemed simple enough, a perfectly ordinary beat.

"'Yes, I see,' I said, 'and the gun stands here.' And I pointed to a place ahead of the unicorn, to which the semi-circle of beaters was moving.

"'No,' he said. 'That would do for any other animal; but not for the unicorn. It's been tried, and that's why nobody ever gets one. With the unicorn avoidance of man amounts to a passion. Whatever it was in the past, that's what it is now; and not to take account of that is an error as great as supposing a rhino can't smell. The moment the unicorn sees the line of beaters, with the flanks coming quietly in on him he knows what's up; he knows he's being driven. By a glance at the line (and his sight is very acute) he knows to what direction. He immediately slips through the forest in exactly the opposite; straight through the line of beaters; and in these forests he usually gets through without even being seen by a native. Not that they haven't seen them.'

"'Then the place for a gun to stand,' I said.

"'Exactly,' he interrupted. 'Stand in front of the unicorn, wherever he is, and we'll try to drive him away from you. He's sure to come straight back.'

"Now this seemed to me perfectly sound. Unicorns do avoid men, there can be no doubt of that. They must have some method in doing it. Granting a considerable intelligence, without which no method is any good, what better than hiding in a dense forest, and, when driven, always going in the opposite direction to that which is obviously intended. And history is too full of the unicorn for us to suppose that they are merely not there.

"'Well,' said Rhino, for Rhino Parks was his name there, whatever it may have been in England once, 'those Wakamba trackers have found him. What about trying tomorrow?'

"'I'm not sure that I can hold a rifle just yet,' I said.

"'No use giving in to malaria here,' he answered, 'or no one would ever do anything.'

"Which is true, though the place is a good deal written up as a health-resort.

"'All right. Tomorrow,' I said.

"And tomorrow came, which was one thing to the good. You never know what's coming, with malaria.

"Well I was up and ready by five, but Rhino wouldn't start till I'd had a good breakfast. So I sat down to it. It had to be liquid, because I could have no more eaten bacon and eggs, as I was just then, than I could have eaten a live squirrel. But we made a breakfast of sorts on two bottles of vermuth that we had; and by about seven we started.

"And now comes the incredible part of my story: we crossed the river and pushed into the forest, and I took up my place where the Wakambas told me in whispers, and the beaters moved off away from me, and all the while I had forgotten to load my rifle. You may not believe me; and, if you don't, I don't wonder; but there it was, I did it. Malaria I suppose. As a matter of fact it is just one of those things that people do do once in their lives, and very often of course it happens to be the last thing they ever do. Well, I stood there with my rifle empty, waiting for the unicorn, a .360 magazine: the magazine holds five cartridges, and there should be another one in the barrel: and the steps of the beaters sounded further and further away from me. And then there came a broken furtive sound, as of something heavy but sly coming down through the forest. And there I was, with my empty rifle ready. And all of a sudden I saw a great shoulder so graceful, so silken and gleaming white, close by in that denseness of greenery, that I knew that it must be the unicorn. Of course I'd seen hundreds of pictures of them, and the thing that I marvelled at most was that the beast, or all I could see of him, was so surprisingly like to the pictures. I put up my rifle and took a good enough aim, and then click, and I knew it was empty.

"Of course I hadn't forgotten to bring any cartridges at all, I wasn't so crazy as that, whatever my temperature was: my pocket was full of them. I put my hand to my pocket and slipped in a cartridge at once, and there I was loaded, with the unicorn still only twenty-five yards away. But he had heard the click, and, whether or not he knew what it was, he at any rate knew it for man, even if he hadn't yet seen me; and he changed at once his slow slinking glide for a sharp trot through the forest. Again in a gap I saw a flash of his whiteness, and I fired and am sure I hit him, and then he came for me. Where I hit him I never knew, my one good chance of a shot behind the shoulder was gone, and I had had to take whatever shot I could get; and now I was again unloaded, for there had been no time to put anything into the magazine, and the unicorn was practically on top of me. Even as I took another cartridge out of my pocket he made a lunge at me with his flashing horn, a deadly weapon of ivory. I parried it with my rifle, and only barely parried, for the strength of its neck was enormous. It wasn't a thing that you could waft aside as you can with the thrust of a sword, if only you are in time; it was so gigantic a thrust that it took all one's strength to turn it. And you had to be just as quick as when trying to parry a rapier; even quicker. At once he lunged again, and again I parried: no question of thinking of trying to load my rifle; there was only just time for the parry. And as I barely parried, and the horn slipped by under my left arm, through the brown shirt I was wearing, clean as a bullet, I knew that I should parry few more, if any, like that; and that with the next thrust, or the one after, all would be over; for the power I felt in that horn was clearly more than my match. So I stepped back to gain an instant; which I barely did, so swiftly the huge beast stepped forward; and then I swung my rifle over my back and before he thrust again I brought it down as hard as I could at his head. I knew it for my last chance, and put into it all the strength that malaria had left me. Now it was his turn to parry. He saw it coming and flicked at it with his horn, and the horn caught it and the two blows came together. Either of them was a good blow. And together they amounted to pretty much of a smash. Well, neither ivory nor steel is unbreakable; and as for the stock of my rifle I don't know where it went: the branches all round were full of flying splinters. And then I saw that long thin murderous horn lying white on the ground beside me. The unicorn saw it too: it put its forefeet out, and lowered its nose and sniffed at it. As the beast was doing nothing at the moment, I picked the horn up. And when it saw the horn in my hand it looked irresolutely at me. For a moment we stood like that. It might easily have overcome me by sheer weight, and trampled me under with its pointed hooves; and yet it stood there motionless, seeming to have an awe for its own horn, which it now saw turned against it. Then I moved the horn into the hand that was holding the rifle, with the intention of seeing if it was possible to get a cartridge into what was left of the breech; and at the movement of the horn in my hand the unicorn shied like a horse, then turned round and kicked out with his heels and sprang away, and was almost immediately lost to sight in the forest. And that was the last I ever saw of a unicorn."

"But the horn," said the young fellow who had asked at first about unicorns. "Why didn't you keep the horn?"

"Waiter," said Jorkens without a word to his critic, "bring me that toasting fork that I gave to the Club."

We most of us present something to the Club, and sure enough Jorkens had once given an ivory-handled toasting fork, that lay in a drawer in the pantry; for whoever wants to use a toasting fork in a Club? And now the waiter brought it, a fork with silver prongs, or electro-plate, and a long ivory handle, too narrow for the tusk of an elephant and too long for a tooth. "And bring me," he said, "a small whiskey and soda."

The whiskey was brought, and as he drank it the strange fork was handed round. Not all of us had seen it before; none of us had eyed it attentively.

"Well, what do you make of it?" said Jorkens when he had finished his whiskey.

It was then that Terbut leaned over to me and whispered, but only too audibly, the one word "Bonzoline."

The ungenerous comment cast over the table something like, well, a miasma. And that's the kind of thing that Jorkens has to put up with.

Ozymandias

There's a member of our Club called Malken, who has made a good deal of money somehow, and I imagine that those of us who were in the club on the afternoon that I tell of didn't seem as though we knew it. At any rate he suddenly asked one of us: "When one gives a dinner-party, how many salt-cellars ought one to have on the table? Do you know what is the right number?"

Of course the question came, "How many diners?" And he was able to answer, "Eighteen."

It was a harmless little piece of ostentation, and the member that he addressed was about to answer, when Jorkens, as widely awake as I have seen him just after lunch, broke in, though he had not been asked, with a keenly judicial air. "In any of the minuter matters of the etiquette of the table," said Jorkens, "I think I can always give you the right answer. The number is not obligatory, not being rigidly fixed, but determined solely by convenience. At a dinner-party of eighteen . . ." But we interrupted Jorkens. "Etiquette?" we said. For we looked on Jorkens as a rough and ready old traveller, who had dined more off packing cases than at tables that held eighteen.

"I knew a man once," Jorkens said, "that was a slave to etiquette. He was addicted to it. And in the end it did him no good. It's curious what things men will take to. It was a curious story altogether."

And so the matter of the eighteen diners was altogether forgotten, and we heard Jorkens' story instead.

"He was a man called Pursker, married, and two sons and a daughter; all grown up, at any rate so they said; but I think you could only have called John and Alice grown up, the eldest and the youngest of the family. Pursker was very well off indeed and had a very nice house in Surrey, when first you looked at it; everything in it was nice, at first sight; but after a while you began to see that it was a kind of dreadful temple to The Thing That Was Done, and that the dining-room table was nothing more than an altar to the things that the Best People did. I came to see a good deal of Pursker at one time, and that's how I got to know such an awful lot about etiquette. You might think that it was trivial and didn't matter much. But the long and the short of it was it mattered so much that there was nothing whatever that Pursker could do, that he might happen to want. He might for instance one day want a bit of bread and cheese after a hard game of tennis, but he no more dared have it than he dared break into a bank. He might like to have dinner at seven and to go to bed early, but the best people dined at 8:30. He might be bitten on the head by a mosquito and want to scratch, he might want to go for a day to Margate or have a walk on Hampstead Heath, he might like to have beer for dinner, he might like on a hot summer's day to sit in his shirt-sleeves, he might like to put on slippers in the evening, he might like to smoke a pipe; but he dared do none of these things, and, if he had, his family wouldn't have let him. There were very few things that Pursker was likely to wish for naturally, that it was right for Pursker to do by that code; or for any of them; but especially Pursker. Especially Pursker, because there was something back in the past that he was hiding; one soon came to see that; Pursker was carrying some weight that none of the rest was carrying. You saw that by the way he steered the conversation. If a family has a skeleton in a cupboard, that family would be apt to discourage guests from wandering down one passage. In the same way Pursker would always discourage me if I ever approached the past. I don't say his wife wouldn't help him to steer conversation away, but I thought that she didn't know what the skeleton was. So, evidently, it was hidden a long way back. She was a dull woman, and weary, wearied in all probability by all that etiquette, which I began to think was itself the cupboard that covered the skeleton. The eldest boy, about twenty-two, seemed human, and especially the girl Alice, about nineteen, but the second boy, Sam, was rabid for their etiquette and all that.

"I got to know Pursker through talking about my travels, as you may perhaps have heard me do at one time or another. That was another curious thing about him, he loved to hear of my past (and of places that I had been to), though he would never speak of his own. Aden was one place that he would always light up at, and Port Said another; and he would want to hear more of them; but if one asked had he been there, the most he would say would be that he had read of them. Why he entertained so much as he did, if he wanted to be so secretive, I could never understand; but we are going in a circle now, the etiquette was necessary somehow to cover up that old skeleton, and the etiquette made them entertain.

"I don't want you to think his family exactly bullied him: they certainly drove him all they could to build up the cupboard and strengthen it, but they lent willing hands of their own, and he was the only one that knew what was in the cupboard.

"I often went to his house: I lived not far off in those days. I'll tell you what happened one autumnal day, when they were giving a large dinner-party. I wasn't dining with them but I'd been to tea, and I stayed late in the hope that I might be able to help, and at the risk of butting in, because there was something strange in the air. I liked the old fellow and I wanted to help him, and the strangeness gradually took shape, till it seemed to amount to this: all the family felt they must give a dinner-party, except Sam, who felt that the danger of doing so just then was far too menacing, and was reproaching his father for giving one anywhere near that date; and his fears had spread to the others. Of what his fears were I had no idea for an hour, nor at any time, until they were suddenly certainties. After long talk, and allusions utterly veiled from me, mainly about the time of year and all the leaves turning, Sam went away to the smoking-room. Thither I followed him, and noticed him looking frequently out of the window, not only at the wide landscape of goldening elms, but far more particularly along the drive, wherever unsheltered parts of it were visible from that room: the drive was pretty thickly lined with yews and not many patches were visible. And so he searched and searched, till his face went suddenly grey, and I saw that his fears, whatever they were, were true. We had been speaking seldom, and now he wouldn't say a word at all. I would have got him to drink a whiskey with me, only I knew their damned rules too well: the right thing to drink before dinner was a sherry, so sherries it had to be, and when they came I made him drink mine as well; and he wanted it; and somehow or other I managed to get a third one into him, and then he talked. And this was what it was all about. His father knew two men that were not the best people, in fact they were common seamen; and these two old fellows, grimy and dressed in the ordinary clothes of their calling, with a huge sea-chest that they always carried between them, would come to the house once a year, and always about the day when the leaves were just turning. When they came they stayed to dine, and then to sleep, and would not be put off, and must have some hold on his father. What it was he daren't guess. He told me about it now because I was bound to see them. He had repeatedly warned his father and mother that they were likely to come about now, but they had thought they would come later and gone blindly on with the getting up of their dinner-party, and when the leaves were actually turning they had said it was too late to cancel it, and that the risk was not so great as Sam made out. There were twenty people coming to dinner, and these two men would sit down amongst them all, and his father daren't stop them. What could be done?

"And as he said this I saw the two old men coming up the drive: they weren't carrying their old sea-chest; one was dragging it by a rope and the other was pushing. For a moment I had had a suggestion hovering upon my lips that they should be put into evening dress. The moment I saw them I knew it was quite impossible. For another fraction of time I wondered if they could possibly be explained as being on their way to a fancy dress ball. But it was quite out of the question; they were too obviously just what they were. So obviously that I gave up thinking. There are people whom explanations can sweep away, but neither of these was of that kind. A man with a short black fringe of whiskers all round his face was pulling the old chest roaring up the gravel, and a man with a stumpy beard of yellowy red was pushing it from behind. Both had their faces so salted with years of spray, that the grit and black oil of engines deep in the seams of them looked as though no number of baths would ever move them now. I gave up thinking because I had no help to offer, and not because I had gone over to the enemy, though I must say that at first sight of the old fellows approaching that custom-ridden house they seemed to be coming like a breeze from the sea into a room whose windows had been shut all through the summer. But to Sam you could see they were more like some fatal draught blowing in on an orchid. And when he saw that I had no help to give him he suddenly came to some sort of a resolution, for his terrified face tautened and, with nothing said to me that one could clearly hear, he strode out of the room.

"What he did I heard afterwards. How much the three sherries had helped him I don't know. But he went to his elder brother and put it to him that this blackmail must stop now; that, whatever their father had done and whatever publicity these two sailors might make if thrown out, nothing they could do would be worse than the impending exposure at a dinner-party to twenty people, and pretty well the pick of the neighbourhood too; for he called it an exposure to have these hangers-on of their father sitting down at that table with them in the sight of all those guests. Etiquette and all that had never sunk quite so deeply into John as it had into Sam and he was for protecting his father's secret, whatever it was, and not angering the two seafarers, and letting them eat with all the rest if they wanted to, and as they certainly would; but all his arguments were swept away before Sam's indignation, and perhaps by the three sherries. Alice was in the room too, and young Boleby: I haven't told you about him. Young Boleby had with a good deal of difficulty got an invitation to that dinner for twenty, and had come an hour too early. You may guess why he came so early. Engaged? No, he wasn't engaged: that was the trouble. He was a farmer, and probably well enough off to have given it up, but he loved farming and everything about it; the sounds of it, even the smells of it; and the feel of the weather that blessed it or threatened it, blowing over the fields that he knew, till they turned mysterious at evening. And a farmer wasn't quite good enough for Alice, and he wouldn't work at anything else. So that was the trouble; all made of course by their etiquette, like all their other troubles. He was for letting the seafarers stop to dinner; but, as he had barely got there himself, you may imagine that his opinion had not much weight, Sam thinking that he had shown a good deal of forbearance in letting him express it at all. If they had been allowed to vote, it would have been three to one against doing what Sam did; but Sam got his way. I could see that, as I came into the room; their conference was just at an end and I could see that Sam had won. If those sherries that I had administered had had anything to do with it, I am sorry. Well, almost on my heels, in walked the two old fellows. They had left their great chest in the hall, or outside the house. They were called Bill and Joe. I got that from the few and brief remarks that the family made to them, and gathered then that Sam and the rest did not know what their surnames were, or they would have used them in all formality. The dark one was Bill, and the red one Joe.

"'Why! There be Miss Alice,' said Bill as he entered the room. 'Grown. Ain't she?' he said to Joe.

"'Like a scarlet runner,' Joe answered.

"'And Master John,' said Bill.

"'And Master Sam,' said Joe quickly, under the frightfully mistaken notion that Sam would be hurt at not being greeted as soon as his brother.

"'And the old un?' said Bill turning to Sam.

"Something in the frigidity of Sam's answer showed Bill that Sam didn't like his father being enquired for in that way.

"'Not old to us of course,' Bill added; 'but we're all old to you young folk.'

"'Like Methuselah,' put in Joe.

"I tried to laugh at Joe's pleasantry, as nobody else did. You ought to laugh at jokes that aren't funny: the others can look after themselves. But I couldn't do it. The damp chill of the welcome of the old seamen was too much for a laugh to live in.

"And then Alice introduced to them young Ned Boleby. Bill turned to Joe and winked. Of course I could see these people's difficulty in setting the two men down to eat at a party that they had made up their minds must be as smart as a reverence for smartness, and plenty of money, could make it. There were certainly difficulties in the situation.

"Then in walked Pursker with his old grey moustache. I can see him still, against the background of his family's disapproval, like a ghost in the damp. He was obviously glad to see Bill and Joe again, as they were to see him, but he clearly could not deal with the situation.

"And then Alice and her young man and John closed in on old Pursker and me; while Sam, with the kind of suggestions that unskilled playwrights use when they want to get one of their characters off the stage, got Bill and Joe out of the room and followed them into the hall.

"The earliest guests arriving must have met those men in the drive; but it is one thing to see that class of man in the grounds of a nice house, and quite another to see them sitting beside you at dinner. And those two never came in. I had heard the grunt of their old sea-chest going grumbling away down the drive, as I prepared to leave myself, but nobody seems to have heard it in the drawing-room. Pursker and Mrs. Pursker wore a look on their faces such as you see on the faces of rabbits down in a burrow when a ferret is loose inside. No, I forgot; you've not had the opportunity of being there; but you know what I mean. Sam, I suppose, wore a look of quiet satisfaction, probably all through dinner; but nobody except him knew quite what had happened, and he hadn't had time to tell before the guests began to arrive.

"I wasn't at the dinner. I gathered that the uneasiness weighing down upon host and hostess affected the whole party, which is odd when you think that they must all have been feeling a fear of which their reason said never a word. But there it was. After the ladies had gone to the drawing-room, but I think before the men joined them, Sam found some opportunity to get his father out of the room (I don't know how he managed it) to tell him the news that he could keep to himself no longer, the news that by an extraordinarily clever document, that he had drawn up himself and persuaded the two men to sign, all avenues to blackmail were closed and the seamen were gone for ever. He seems to have waited for his father to praise him; and he waited a long time, while the old man never spoke.

"At last he said, 'Gone!'

"And Sam said, 'Gone, all right.'

"And after a while old Pursker began to speak.

"'Do you know that it takes ten thousand a year to run this place as we run it?'

"'Well, you've got it, haven't you?' said Sam.

"'I had it last year. And for many years,' answered Pursker. 'Do you know how it comes?'

"'From the Bank, I suppose,' Sam answered.

"'No,' said Pursker.

"'Well, tell me,' said Sam.

"'In that box.'

"'In that box?'

"'Yes, that box that they always bring with them.'

"'That old sea-chest?' said Sam.

"'It's full of gold pieces,' said his father. 'Full to the brim. As large round,' and he very nearly sobbed as he said it, 'as large round as oyster-shells.'

"And then they talked over details for a bit, such as that the two seafarers had no known address, but came and went like the swallows. That was the old man's contribution to the discussion, while the young man had to contribute as his share the certainty that the two old fellows would never come again. He had made about as sure enough of that as any man can make sure of anything, and had been taking credit for the thoroughness of his foresight for about an hour and a half. A little while after that, when the guests were gone, there had been a family conclave, and the skeleton walked out of the cupboard; and within a week or so the cupboard collapsed after it. I mean all the ceremonious pomposity, the fashion and all the rest of it, that had concealed the skeleton, disappeared when it rattled its bones for the first time before the eyes of Mrs. Pursker and her three children. And the skeleton was simply this; Jim Pursker Esquire had once been a common seaman. He had not only been a friend and contemporary of Bill and Joe, but a colleague and a collaborator.

"I don't think Mrs. Pursker had realized it at first. As far as I can make out she did not in the least understand, until Mr. Pursker uttered one remark that made the whole thing ruthlessly clear, and she saw the situation with one shock all in a moment. 'I used to chew tobacco,' he said.

"In the silence that followed that he had explained how he saved up his money, while others spent theirs on drink, till he had £500; and how Bill and Joe and another man had a tale of buried treasure, and used to whisper and plan about it, and it was the guiding star of their lives. And it was true: it was there. Of course they wouldn't say where; they couldn't; they were bound by oath. And Pursker had believed in them and backed them with all his money, and got a fourth share of it, until Jack Smith had died and then he had a third. Bill and Joe used to bring away as much as two men could manage, without letting any other man into it, on mules once a year. And ten thousand pounds worth of these great Spanish gold pieces was Pursker's share. Now it was gone."

"And had he nothing invested?" said Malken.

"Hardly anything," Jorkens replied. "The buried treasure was his investment. He knew there was plenty of it, and it was all arranged that when Bill or Joe died he should come into his share too. I forget which. One of them had dependants of his own and the other hadn't. Anyhow Pursker felt he was well provided for."

Malken snorted at that sort of financial method, and Jorkens continued: "And they'd a curious arrangement that I'll tell you about later, whereby Jack Smith had had one clue as to where the place was, and old Pursker another, while Bill and Joe had written out a third clue, of little value in itself and meaning nothing to anyone that might steal it, only of value to the rightful heir; that is to say to the man that had the other two clues. As a matter of fact this clue of Bill and Joe was never found by anyone."

"More sense in that," said Malken. "That's like three men having each a key to a safe, that will only unlock with all three."

"Exactly," said Jorkens. "The first clue Pursker remembered, but seemed to have little use for, it was lying about the house somewhere, like one of those keys of old boxes one never uses; the second had to be sought for; and the third, which there was no finding, had to be hammered out afresh by human wits. But they'd no thought of clues for the next two weeks. I often went and saw them: it was the least I could do after all the times that they'd entertained me, and I thought I might be some use. But I couldn't be. The whole house was like a camp in a dust-storm. Everything upside down and, in addition to that, every one of them in each other's way, and all tumbling over boxes and drifting pieces of furniture. It was a mournful sight. There's a time to sell, and a way of selling, nice furniture and good pictures, and there's a way of selling houses too: they sold at the wrong time and in the wrong way. They got only twenty-five thousand for everything, including their bit of land. Five per cent went to the auctioneer, and Pursker owed a few thousand, as he well might, expecting his dividend of ten thousand when he did; and then there were taxes: he barely invested eighteen thousand, at four per cent, which was all you could get in those days without speculation. With taxes again, that brought him little more than six hundred a year. He may have had two hundred a year more from the few investments he'd made, but that all went in pensions and other commitments to his workmen and various dependants. I think he gave fifty pounds a year each to the boys, a hundred a year to his wife, for herself and Alice, and four hundred a year was all he had left to keep him for the rest of his life. On this they took a house somewhere in Sydenham; I needn't say it was small. It was not till they settled into their dingy house that I could get them to listen to any advice from me; they were too busy falling with their shattered fortunes. But when they'd been there a few days I came and advised them. Well, I'll admit that my theories all turned out to be wrong, so that the advice I gave may not in a way have been valuable. But I often think that when someone's advising a family it stimulates their own wits, and at any rate they like to think that somebody's taking trouble about them. And that's the way it affected the Purskers. Or perhaps I should say Ned Boleby, for the Purskers' wits seemed still to remain numb after weeks. It was Ned that began to have theories to set against mine. I like to think that his ideas might not have come to him if I had not started him off with mine, even though mine might not have turned out to be of any use in themselves. In fact they weren't.

"Ned Boleby was no better off than he was before. They had had their lesson, and given up etiquette and all that stuff; but they wanted to save one thing out of the wreck, and that was to see Alice do well for herself, and they thought the young farmer had not quite enough for her. If they could have given him something, to make it enough, they would have; but they hadn't got it now. So he was just where he was before. It was an odd line for them to take up, for Boleby was probably richer than Pursker now, but the only hope that old Pursker had left was to see his daughter free of all the worries that he was beginning to detect hovering over four hundred a year. Boleby probably made a clear five hundred.

"Now Boleby from the start of this new life of the Purskers had large and thriving hopes, and it was he who first made Pursker find his clue to the place of the treasure. This Pursker with some difficulty did, and brought it to the new house with him. It was a photograph of a man apparently an Englishman, at any rate the cut of his breeches and the leggings he wore looked familiar, standing with folded arms, and legs rather wide apart, on the top of a low ridge in what was evidently a desert, and there was a cross marked on the ground in ink at his feet. His face too was familiar enough; you would have said a minor clerk in an English bank, having his holiday; except for that rather odd attitude; that was the only curious thing about him; the wide legs, the folded arms, and the head sunk forward as though he brooded alone, but for the cheery face that rather suggested cricket than lonely contemplation. Boleby got the thing enlarged and hung up in the drawing-room, and it was there that I first saw it, over the mantelpiece. It wasn't much good, for the desert was utterly featureless, a flat expanse with a man standing in it, and nothing special about the man; but there couldn't be much doubt that the cross marked the place of the treasure, and that seemed some sort of comfort, though there was no possible way of seeing where that was, except that it was in a desert. One couldn't even tell which desert.

"Well, while Boleby only got them to hang the enlargement up so as to have something to turn their hopes to every day, and to keep their spirits from falling as low as their fortunes, he himself was constantly studying it; and if there'd been any feature whatever in the landscape I believe he'd have located the desert, but unfortunately there was nothing, for the bit of a ridge the man stood on couldn't be called a feature. So one day he said: 'We must get hold of the other clue. The one Jack Smith had.'

"It was very difficult to get anything out of Pursker. 'What was Jack Smith's address?' Boleby asked him.

"'He's dead,' said Pursker.

"'Yes, I know,' said Boleby, 'but where used he to live?'

"'I don't know,' said Pursker.

"And yet it turned out that Pursker had a letter from him.

"'When you had his share,' said Boleby, 'you should have had his clue.'

"'I think his landlady kept his papers,' said Pursker listlessly.

"Well, the address on the letter was a lodging house in Swanley. And off went Boleby leaving a light like hope in the eyes of Alice, and the rest too abject to care.

"And the wonderful thing was that Boleby found it. He came back in about a week with a square of paper exactly the same size as the one with the photograph, and a cross marked on the paper in the same spot as what it was in the photograph, only the paper was otherwise perfectly blank. But on the back was clearly written:

That was the second clue.

"From the look in the grey eyes of Alice when Ned Boleby came with the clue, you would have thought that it was the only clue they needed, the only key to the safe, as you put it, Malken. But it was one of three, and they only had two, and this one was pretty rusty, for unless their wits could polish it up a bit it had no meaning at all. I was there when he came, and I was the first to look at it. It evidently referred to the photograph: we made quite sure of that by placing one over the other and putting a pin through, and it went right through the centre of the cross on each. I said at first that the N stood for North, and 5 and 11 for the latitude and the longitude. The mark after the 12 I took for an inverted comma, meaning that they were quoting somebody; and I certainly took too many of the numbers as being suggestions for digging. Well, I won't trouble you with my theories, because, as I told you, they turned out to be wrong, yet I hope they had their uses. It should not be forgotten how much the loser contributes to almost any game. And I may add that my suggestions were much better than any of the Purskers made. It was only Boleby that showed an uncanny knack of getting hold of the sense of it. Even now, when I know what it means, I often wonder how he ever made head or tail of it; and he wouldn't have done if it hadn't been for one comma. It was that 'Dig 3' that helped him. 'That is obviously 3 feet,' he said. And we all agreed to that.

"'Then the little mark after the 12' (which was not very clear) 'must mean feet as well,' said Boleby. And from that he went on, going backwards. Getting the 12 feet sort of uncovered the next bunch of numbers. '23.12.4 is a date,' he said. 'The 23rd of December, 1904.' And from dates, after a little talk, he came to time. '12.5 is the hour,' he said, 'the hour that the photograph was taken. And the 12 feet would be the distance from the camera, which, as one can see, is about what it is.'

"'But what's J. N.?' said Sam, a bit jealous of the speed with which Boleby was getting on.

"'The initials of the man in the photograph,' said Boleby at once. 'We don't know who he was and probably never shall. I don't suppose he mattered very much. We've no record of a fifth man in it, so I doubt very much if they ever let him know that he was standing over the treasure, or that there was any treasure at all.'

"'Then what's he there for?' said Sam.

"'As a mark,' said Boleby.

"'But unless he's standing there still,' said Sam, 'what's the use of a mark in a perfectly flat desert?'

"There was no answering that, and if Sam had been contented with the last word he'd have scored, as he intended to, but he must needs blurt out, 'And what's 5.11?'

"Boleby hadn't thought of that, but now it was so obviously J. N.'s height, as he told Sam at once, and that made him surer than ever that J. N. was a mark, though it was long before he guessed what on earth was the use of a movable mark in a desert. I went away after that and turned over for long in my mind what the two clues seemed to be saying, and I could only make it out that they said, if you put a five-foot-eleven man with his feet apart in a desert at 12.5p.m. (for there'd be no sunlight at 12.5a.m.), the treasure will be between his feet, three feet down. The Purskers had given up hope again, and there seemed to me nothing to be got out of it, but Boleby kept on.

"I went back to see them next day, more to see if they were getting over their hopelessness than from any idea that there was anything more to be done towards getting a sight of their treasure. And I hadn't been there long when Ned Boleby came bursting into the room, in which all the family were, with me trying to cheer them up; he'd been sitting up half the night and was full of ideas.

"'Look here,' he said as he came into the room. 'Look at that shadow.' And he held out the original photograph, a little thing of five inches by four. 'What time of year would you say that was?'

"I glanced at it. 'Why, midsummer,' I said.

"'And the date,' he said.

"'Why yes,' I said, 'December. You've got the date wrong.'

"Without taking any notice of my remark he spun round and asked for an atlas, and Alice got him one and he opened it and found a map of the world, a Mercator's projection. Then he made some charcoal for himself by burning the end of a pencil. 'I've narrowed it down a bit,' he said. 'It's not in Russia,' and he began to blacken Russia out.

"'But what are you messing the map for?' said Sam.

"'And it's not in China,' he said, and he blackened out China. 'Or anywhere in Europe.' And out Europe went. And they seemed to believe him, and a gleam came to the wan faces of the old couple.

"'And it's not in the United States of America,' he added, 'or Canada.'

"'But why? Why?' asked Mrs. Pursker.

"'Because it's not in the Northern hemisphere at all,' said Boleby. 'Look at that shadow.'

"And we all looked up at the enlargement over the mantelpiece where the shadow of the young man standing with folded arms was as squat as a shadow can be. 'And look at the date,' he said. 'That must be very nearly under the sun when it's vertical, and where's the sun in December? Why down along the tropic of Capricorn.'

"'Why, that's so,' I said.

"And then he began to blacken out the whole south of the world and a bit along the equator, until only a strip of the map was left, which would have been about a thousand miles wide, with the dotted line of Capricorn running along the middle of it, and most of it was over the sea. 'And we'll narrow down that belt a lot,' he said, 'when we get scientific assistance.'

"Pursker looked merely dazed, but, from then on, hope began to come back to that family. It showed itself by a flood of talk. A bright suggestion had brought back hope to them; and they all poured out a flood of suggestions, not that any of them were of any use; but the talk was bright, almost feverish. There was no real use in narrowing it down to a belt across the world, when all you had to guide you was a sandy ridge of rock on which the bank clerk was standing, a ridge in no way different from millions of others, and with no landmark whatever to locate it. Boleby admitted all this, but they clung to their new hope. 'No,' said Boleby, 'we want something more. I doubt if there are large deserts like this in South America. Capricorn passes through a fairly narrow part of South Africa; we might search that in five years. But the whole width of Australia beats us; and most of it desert, I fancy, where Capricorn goes.'

"'Couldn't we try?' said Alice.

"'Absolutely hopeless,' said Boleby. 'You wouldn't notice that ridge at three hundred yards. Have you nothing more of Jack Smith's except that one letter that said nothing?'

"'He gave Father a book once,' said Sam.

"'What kind of book?' Boleby asked him.

"'A book of poetry, I think,' said Sam. 'He read poetry.'

"'Let's see it,' said Boleby.

"Even now Sam showed a trace of some sort of scorn as he went to get the book, and returned with it smiling and gave it to Boleby. It was a 'Golden Treasury,' and Jack Smith had sent it to Pursker before he died. With all of them watching him Boleby had to open the pages, now that he had sent for the book. He turned them over, trying to conceal the futility of it, and found nothing of any use; when, turning the pages as the left thumb turns them, he came to the first page of all. And there was an inscription in the hand of Jack Smith: 'I met a traveller from an antique land.' That was all. At first Boleby read it to himself, then mumbled it partly aloud, and still saw nothing.

"And suddenly he shouted: 'I have it!'

"They all looked up expectant.

"'An antique land,' he shouted.

"'Egypt,' I said at once. And, mind you, Egypt for certain's the setting of Shelley's sonnet.

"'No,' he said.

"'It couldn't very well have been anywhere else,' I told him.

"'What was the sonnet about?' he asked me.

"'About a colossus,' said I.

"'And that's what we've got to look for,' said Boleby. 'It knocks out the whole of Australia. Nobody ever built in that size there until we went there, and we don't build colossi. It's in Africa, not far from the line of Capricorn, and we ought to be able to find it.'

"'But why? Why?' urged everyone.

"And Sam said, 'A mere quotation from Shelley doesn't prove it.'

"'Prove it! No,' said Boleby. 'It isn't proof; it's a hint.'

"'I can't see what it hints,' Sam went on.

"'Look at that attitude,' said Boleby, pointing toward the photograph.

"'Napoleon,' said somebody.

"'Well, and look at that face,' went on Boleby.

"'Oh, mild,' I said.

"'Then, why was that sort of man striking that attitude?' Boleby asked us, and went on: 'To fit in. And against what? Don't you see now? There is a featureless desert with a man in it. And a photograph of it is treasured to mark an incredibly valuable site. As you can see nothing at all to distinguish it from any other arid part of the earth when the man's there, the identifying feature must be behind him. But I couldn't think what. Now it's as clear as daylight. The treasure is where a man of five-foot-eleven exactly conceals the colossus, limb for limb.' Sam whistled. 'It must be rather like the colossus of Rhodes,' Boleby continued, 'for you see how the man is standing. You see how he has even taken his hat off to get the head right, pretty dangerous in that sun. It's probably some vast thing. Probably the whole desert is dominated by it. We've got to find a spot in that desert where twelve feet away from a five-foot-eleven man on a ridge, and looking towards the colossus, you can see nothing at all, and of course with nothing of the man left over; for his odd attitude would be meaningless if he was not exactly eclipsing the figure, with nothing to spare.'

"'And how do you know which side of the colossus he is?' said Pursker, beginning to believe in it all, yet hardly daring yet to think it quite true.

"'By the way the shadow goes, such as it is,' said Boleby.

"And we looked up and could just distinguish that the squat shadow was coming towards you, and if anything a little towards the right.

"And Boleby went on: 'Well, a thing like that should be easy enough to find. Anyone within thirty miles of it should have heard of it; so that even if we had to go right across Africa we should leave a strip of sixty miles, that's thirty miles left and right of us, in which we could say for certain that the colossus was not, if we met nobody who had heard of it. The journey back would make it a hundred and twenty; do the double journey again, and we should have about covered the strip along which a shadow could look anything like that at noon in December.'

"They were gazing at him in silence.

"'Cost a bit,' I said.

"'But we shan't have to go right across,' said Boleby. 'Remember that this treasure is a sailor's yarn, and the odds are that it's under a hundred miles from the coast. Well, what do you think of it?' he said to me.

"'Sounds to me like wedding bells,' I said.

"And sure enough it was. Ned Boleby and Alice were married within the year; and within the year the whole family were back at their old place, giving larger dinner parties than ever, and with every bit of the old ceremony. I often guessed what happened. I never knew for certain that it was in Africa at all. You see, it all depends on whether there are any deserts to be found in South America. And then it might be an island; but precious few besides Madagascar; the tropic of Capricorn is almost all in the water.

"Of course I never dreamed of going to see for myself: too many people there before me.

"I asked Alice about it once when I met her, very smart; but, I will say, very happy; at the opening day of the Royal Academy. I chose a fleeting moment while nobody was in ear-shot, and said: 'Where was Ozymandias?' You remember the big boy of Shelley's sonnet.

"And she said: 'What with this and Ascot and Goodwood, and dining out so much, and then the garden parties, and one thing and another.'

"'Yes I know,' I said, for hundreds of yards of that season's draperies were bearing down on us, and I wanted to hear while we couldn't be overheard. 'But where was the treasure?'

"'Papa and the boys,' she said, 'were really so busy that they never found time to go.'

"I think Alice might have trusted me.

"Oh, well. Let's forget her. Waiter!"

At the End of the Universe

Tales that Jorkens has told me, and that I have written down, have now been before the public for some while, and, though doubts about parts of them have been occasionally noticeable, no proof has been even offered, far less established, against the accuracy of any of them. For this reason I feel myself justified in recording the following story, which I hesitated to do while Jorkens' veracity was, as it were, untried.

It was a bleak day in London about the turn of the year, with winter drawing nearer than one was inclined to suspect; and I rather think, looking back on it, that I had had insufficient exercise for over a week, which may have affected one's liver. Whether this was really so I cannot say, I can only give you my symptoms: I felt that much in our political system must be so attractive to the majority of the electorate that the system was bound to be extended, perhaps rapidly; and that, being unsound, it must one of these days crash into some irresistible fact of economics; and I felt that in other directions our power so far exceeded our wisdom that humanity was by no means to be trusted with the bombing plane, or even with electricity, the harm we have done with steam alone being quite enough for one dynasty. So that I saw disaster coming from two directions, and too many willing hands helping it on its way.

I had tried a much advertised cure; you take it in your soup and it is perfectly tasteless; but it only made me worse. As a last resort I dropped into the club, hoping to find Jorkens; and he was there all right, though asleep. So I sat down beside him and called to one of the waiters to bring me a large whiskey; and at the sound of my order Jorkens partially woke; at least he turned his head a little towards me with the words, "That is very good of you," and remained with his eyes shut, quiet in the warmth of the fire, until the whiskey came.

When Jorkens had drunk the large whiskey, with a little compliment to myself that it would not look well for one to repeat here, I turned to him for a story; for I needed distraction from the troubles that threatened humanity, and not only that but I had invested £50 in Bovuela United Railways, and they had recently started a civil war in Bovuela, and I knew they'd tear up the railways, so as to prove to larger islands that they really were having a war. Well, never mind that now. I said to Jorkens, as I had once said before, "What is the strangest thing you have ever seen?" And, as it happened, Jorkens remembered that I had previously asked the same question.

"I've told you," said Jorkens.

"Yes, yes," I said, "the daughter of Rameses. I suppose that was the strangest thing that anyone could have seen."

"Oh, I wouldn't say that," answered Jorkens.

"Not?" said I.

"No," said Jorkens, "for I was once only five yards from a man, in the very same room with him, when he saw a far stranger thing; the most remarkable sight, I should say, that the human eye ever beheld. I wish I'd seen it myself now. I might have, only that I wouldn't trouble to look. That's often the way with things like that."

"Yes, I suppose it is," I said. "But what was it?"

"I'll tell you," said Jorkens. And with a glance round the room to see that Terbut wasn't there, the one man that is Jorkens's bugbear, he told me this story as we sat alone in the club.

"It was some years ago," said Jorkens, "before contract bridge had made any appreciable headway and the old kind was still played, the dealer alone making trumps, and before anything at all was known of the work of Einstein, except to a very few men.

"I was staying with old Hollison, one of the very few: I was a friend of his nephew. You know he used to have a telescope in the hall of his house; of course they've dismantled it long ago, but in its time it was one of the biggest in England. There he used to sit at one end of the hall, gazing up at the stars, while his family and their friends played bridge in the middle. He was always quite quiet they said, and never gave any trouble. And then one day, just before dinner, when I was staying there, about 7.30 of a winter's evening, he suddenly began to quote from the Nunc dimittis: 'Lord, now lettest thou Thy servant depart in peace, for mine eyes have seen.' Of course the bridge-players didn't know what to make of it; but beyond a raised eyebrow and a glance from face to face, and perhaps the barest trace of an answering smile, there was no sign to show they had heard him say anything odd. I heard it too, though I was farther off.

"And then he turned to the young party, two boys and two girls playing bridge, and said: 'I don't know if you would care to see. It's rather . . .'

"But the old man stopped at that, the right words not coming to him. It was his nephew that he seemed to be looking at, a boy of about twenty-four; but he was dealer, and with a flick of his eye he directed the invitation to his partner, who knowing that his hand would go down in a moment, said 'Yes, it would interest me very much.'

"Tuppin was his name, and he got up slowly, waiting for trumps to be declared and the game to commence. Young Scarton; that is the nephew; made trumps at once: nobody doubled, and dummy's cards went down, and he walked over showing an expression of polite interest to the half-partitioned corner where the great telescope was.

"'It's like this,' said old Hollison, full of diffidence, for he knew what his dreams of science seemed to the young. 'We know that matter curves, and the world is round. It seems that light, and that is sight, curves too. So that if we could see to the end of the universe, what should we see?'

"'Well, of course, I don't know,' said Tuppin very politely. 'You see I'm afraid I'm not clever enough.'

"'No,' said old Hollison. 'And of course there might be no end. The thing might have been infinite, so that however far we could see we should never have known the universe, no more than an ant in a field could know of a continent.'

"And at this point Tuppin threw in, 'No, of course not,' without any idea of what was coming.

"'But,' Hollison went on, 'I have been working out something for years, all the time I was increasing the size of my telescopes, so that when I got one large enough I knew at last what to look for. I mightn't have found it; but it's there. The universe is finite.'

"'Is it really?' said Tuppin.

"And I knew from the fervour in Hollison's voice as he said the last four words that Tuppin's remark was altogether inadequate. But the old man went on in spite of it.

"'What I worked on,' he said, 'was the appearance of the constellation in which our sun swims, and of those constellations that are its neighbours, if looked at from a distance beyond your imagination, and from what I may call the other side. It should be something like this.'

"And he handed to Tuppin what the young fellow described to me afterwards as a black post-card with some very faint dots on it. I never knew what became of it.

"'Oh, yes,' said Tuppin with as much interest as he could get into his voice.

"'Now, see if you can see it,' said Hollison, showing the way to his telescope.

"'Hullo,' I said to myself, 'that's something new. It's night and he's looking at the sun. He's seeing the solar system from outside it.'

"It's staggering to think of what Tuppin might have seen; nothing else than the end of the universe; sight coming home from its tour of all that matter, having circumnavigated all that was ever made, the sun seen faint as a star of the thirtieth magnitude, a small pale dot in a constellation of dots on the far side of creation. But at that moment the game was over: I remember Scarton made two tricks in no trumps, and Tuppin, muttering something like, 'I'd be very glad to see it after this rubber,' went back to the others. I think they played one more hand, and then dressed for dinner. And after dinner I remember the moon got in the way; and before next evening came old Hollison died. He had been talking to Tuppin calmly enough, but I think the excitement of what he saw after those years of work had quickened his pulse a good deal, and, having a weak heart, that had been bad for it. At any rate he died, and the party came to an end hurriedly, and no more was ever heard of his amazing discovery. If I could only have seen it I could have told them what to look for. All I can say now is that I was within five yards when that stupendous sight was seen by man, and the universe known to be finite."

"Why didn't you have a look?" I asked. "You said you weren't playing."

"No, I wasn't playing bridge," said Jorkens, "but I was friends with the four that were; and there's one thing nobody's ever called me yet. Nobody's ever called me a highbrow. Had I gone over and seen those stars while the rest were playing bridge, that's what they might have said of me. They were all younger than me, and I should have gradually dropped out from them. And that's a lonely thing. No, I have my faults. Waiter, another whiskey. I have my faults, but nobody's called me a highbrow."

"No, no," I said, "Jorkens, and nobody ever will."

He gripped my hand and thanked me.

The Black Mamba

Lunch was not yet over in the Billiards Club when, chancing to look through the window, I noticed that lights were appearing in other houses; not all at once, but furtively, as though aware that the hour was not yet come for any lesser lights, yet one by one they stole softly into the murkiness, and the darkness deepened around them as they came. It was late November.

These dark months of the winter in London are profitably passed by work, by giving more attention to business, by studying such things as conditions, and in many other ways, but at the Billiards Club we pay concentrated attention to stories of out-of-the-way parts of the world, or out-of-the-way events that one member or another has seen. And at this time of the year we particularly look to such entertainment from Jorkens, with the exception of one or two members who require everything to be proved as though Jorkens were on his trial in a court of law. And now Jorkens was with us, but silent, as he had been for several days, and so morose that he seemed to resent being spoken to; and he was eyeing other members with an attitude so malevolent that I gave up any hope of a story that bleak day, and concentrated instead on trying to get some apology from some of the members for whatever it was that had offended Jorkens. But, as Jorkens wouldn't speak, it was hard to find out who had insulted him.

I began by catching an eye here and an eye there among those at whom he was scowling, and suggesting to them, by a glance at the waiter, that they should offer Jorkens a whiskey. And this two or three of them did, and Jorkens refused them; so, having failed as a peacemaker, I tried to cheer him by offering him one myself. This he refused too: it was before him on a salver and he refused it, and saw it carried away out of the room. Some of us looked at each other, then at Jorkens, but not a glimpse of regret was there on his face, not a hint of recalling the waiter. And then the moroseness that had puzzled us for a fortnight, the trouble that I had so blunderingly tried to put right, was revealed in a single sentence.

"My doctor has forbidden me whiskey," he said.

So that was it. What was to be done next? It was growing darker and darker outside in the cold, and in another five minutes Bettin would tell a story, and that would only make everything worse; a long, long tale full of details, each one made vividly clear by an overwhelming veracity; there would be no turning him aside from it once he started. Could anything stir Jorkens to bring us any glimmer from the lands in which our November is unknown? He sipped at a tumbler of water, and I doubted it. There were many efforts to draw him, but with no success; in answer to some of them he never even grunted.

Then someone, talking of Africa, mentioned Somalis. At that, Jorkens looked up, alert, with his eyes flashing. He had found at last the enemy that his bitter mood needed in that bleak evening. He had no quarrel with any of us; but Somalis, they were the people for whom his fury was raging.

"Somalis!" he said. One word of contemptuous anger.

But one or two of us thought rather well of Somalis, and said so, in spite of Jorkens. In fact, barring the Masai, there is no tribe able to beat them through many a hundred miles of their part of Africa. But Jorkens only repeated their name with the same scorn and fury.

"What have the Somalis ever done to you?" said Terbut. And Jorkens, seeing that he had to defend himself for what we took as an unfair attitude, which was clear enough in his look and his bitter tones, calmed himself in a few moments, and said with a wistfulness I have not often heard in his voice:

"I've only really wanted one thing in my life, and the Somalis wouldn't let me have it."

Somehow the way he said it struck a quiet, even on Terbut, and he said quite gently to Jorkens: "What was it?"

"Sleep," said Jorkens.

"Sleep?" we said, wondering that Jorkens had not wanted many things more.

But Jorkens' eyes were away from us and the fog, looking back far through the past: "The Somalis," he said. "They wouldn't let me sleep."

And somehow or other, when I saw that look on Jorkens' face, I abused the Somalis, of whom I know little enough, and he seemed grateful for my trifling support; and that is how, I think, we got the story, his first word, almost, for a fortnight.

"I was on a safari in East Africa, with a few Somali boys. I had chosen them, as I had been told that they were stouter fellows than the Kikuyus, in whose country I was; stouter indeed than most, and more likely to stick to you, if there was trouble, than almost any others. I had pitched my little camp and was standing just outside it, gazing at the view that I always keep in my memory, even here in this fog; while they finished getting the tents up.

"I was standing by the northern Guaso Nyero, a sluggish stream going through marshes: suddenly it leaps forward, like a fat horse hit by surprise, and roars downward to the very feet of the forest; and up from that raging fall and higher than the marshes from which it came, soar tier upon tier of cedars hugely bearded with moss. One red lily stood five feet high by the brink of the fall. I was looking silently at the scene below me, thinking of the beauty of Creation, when something struck me through my leather boot, in the upper part of the foot; and I knew it for a black mamba. I don't know how I knew it; I don't think I've ever seen one; and it was gone at once through the grasses; but I knew. It is one of the three deadliest snakes in Africa.

"Four of my Somalis were standing quite near, and I shouted to them, 'I think black mamba. Look, see.' And I pointed to the grasses where he had gone. But they only looked at me. Then one of them tied a tourniquet round my leg, which was quite the right thing to do. And one of them ran and got a knife from the camp, and came back with it and cut a bit at my foot. Well, I didn't mind that. And all the while they were watching my face.

"It was time to try my own remedy then, permanganate of potash, that I kept in my tent, thirty yards away. And they helped me there, for I was a bit lame from their cutting. And I began to wonder as I went whether their knife-work and tourniquet and my little permanganate crystals would ever be any use. You see, it was rather near a vein. Well, I sat on my bed and shoved the crystals in; and then, what with their cutting and the infernal permanganate, and the shock of that sudden bite while I was thinking of nothing of the sort, I felt like taking a bit of rest on my bed. They were all of them still looking at me; and as I lay down on the bed they said, 'Black mamba.'

"They had none of them troubled to go and look in the grass where I showed them, but they looked at me now and said, 'Black mamba,' and nodded. Then one of them slipped away: I caught the word 'fire' in their language: and I said to the other three, 'I'll rest a bit now.'

"They looked at one another. They lifted me off the bed, one at each arm. 'Walk,' they said; and we went out of the tent, with the third one coming behind me.

"Well, sick or fit, you can't give way to natives like that, or you'd lose all control over them for ever. So I just turned round to one of them, to put him in his place; and then that great yearning for sleep descended on me in earnest. I didn't speak to him: I left him to do what he liked: I didn't care if I never controlled them again. I didn't care if they dragged a white man about like an old sack of potatoes. I only wanted sleep. When they wouldn't stop walking and dragging me up and down I said: 'All right, I'm going to sleep here. Go on with your walk. I'm going to sleep.'

"I didn't mind. There was a sleepiness on me beyond anything I'd ever known. I didn't care where I slept, so long as I slept deep, and I dropped my head forward and dragged my feet and let them pull me along. I thought to be sound asleep in a couple of minutes. But I hadn't settled down to rest for four of their paces, when the Somali behind me (he was my gun-bearer, too) began to beat me on the calves of my legs, and on the tendon above the heel that they call the tendon Achilles: that hurt infernally. I moved my feet then to keep them out of his way, and so we went on for a while. It wasn't the movement that kept me awake, but what must have been the work of the will, to the extent necessary to move each foot; and after every footstep I hoped to sleep, but the damned fellow behind me never let one step pass, and if I didn't take each footstep he was hammering that bruised tendon with a stick.

"I think all this must have begun at sunset, for I know it was all clear daylight while I was standing watching the falls, but those terrible walks up and down were taken in dwindling light, and soon I saw bright firelight where one of the Somalis was sitting heating an iron. And the hyenas were yelling as they always do in honor of the equatorial sunset. For a while, by hurrying my steps, I kept just ahead of the stick of the man behind; but if I was the least slow, crash came the stick, and that intense pain again, always on the same part of the foot. And darkness all the while was coming on rapidly. But, more rapidly than night on the equator, was coming now a deeper yearning for sleep, so that all at once I saw that pain didn't matter. Let him batter my heels, I thought all of a sudden; let him cut them off; there was only one thing I wanted, and that was sleep. So I let my feet drag again. And I saw then that I was right, pain did not matter, so long as I only had sleep. They shouted then to the man at the fire, sitting beside the cedar-logs, but he seemed not to be ready, and I thought I should beat them and get some sleep. And I very nearly did. They doubled their pace and tried new dodges, but I nearly beat them before the man came with the iron. It was a huge piece of iron, something to do with a wagon, and it wasn't yet ready. Nothing any longer had any interest for me whatever except sleep. Pain no longer mattered, and as for life, I wasn't thinking of the future but only of this one overwhelming need. My brains were growing heavy as gold and lead, but I could still use them. I turned first to the Somali that was holding my left arm. I offered him five head of cattle, and went to ten, before I saw that the damned fellow wouldn't take anything. Ten head of cattle for five minutes sleep. I turned to the other one then, the man that had hold of my right arm, and offered him fantastic numbers of oxen, a hundred of the best cattle in Kenya, to let me sleep for ten minutes. He was no good either. I'd paid them well, and treated them well, and fed them well, and never asked anything of them before; and now I only wanted this one thing. What was life to me? It was sleep I wanted.

"And then the other Somali came with the hot iron. It wasn't so easy to sleep after that. They shoved it into the hole they had cut round the snakebite. I might have got to sleep if they'd stopped at that. But they played all kinds of heathenish games with that iron, things that no right-minded civilized man would think of; and the only chance I had then of trying to get to sleep was whenever he went back to his fire of cedar to heat up the iron again. Damn them, I forgave them the torture; but neither then nor ever, have I forgiven them for frustrating that yearning. Now, don't tell me it was bad for me. I yearned for sleep, and never have I yearned for anything else so much. I hardly thought they could have beaten me; but they did. I hardly thought they had the guts to hold out against my determination, but they beat my will in the end; and at last, when the night was very cold, and Lord knows how late, they brought me all limp to my tent. And there I sat on my bed and took off my half-burned boot, and began to put some ointment and lint on the awful mess they had made of my foot; and, when they saw me interested in this, they left me at last alone. And when I had my foot sufficiently bandaged I undressed and went to bed and got some sleep, but a sleep full of phrases that haven't quite got meanings, and thousands of ideas in a hurry but getting nowhere, and wakeful weary dreams: it was not the sleep that I wanted."

Jorkens gave one long sigh and was mournfully silent.

"Well," said Terbut, "I think you were undeservedly lucky to have such men at a crisis. I never heard of such devotion. You wouldn't be here now, but for them."

"Here," said Jorkens with a world of scorn, and looking out at the fog. "With the pound at twelve shillings, and taxes what they are!"

"It isn't twelve shillings," said Terbut. "It's over fourteen."

"And what does that matter to me," retorted Jorkens bitterly, "when I haven't got any pounds, and not a dividend paying?"

I ordered two whiskeys and sodas from the waiter then.

"I see you've ordered one for me," said Jorkens. "Damn my doctor. I'll have it."

"No, Jorkens," I said, "they are both for you."

And the old light came back into his eye.

Well, that's the end of the story. But there's a certain corroboration, or lack of it, according to how you like to look at it, that I ought to add. Terbut turned to Jorkens and said:

"A bite like that, and such drastic remedies, must have left an awful scar on your foot."

"Yes," said Jorkens. "It did."

"Might we have a look at it?" said Terbut.

"If you like to take my boot of," said Jorkens.

And it certainly was my impression that he stretched out his left foot towards Terbut.

At any rate Terbut took the boot off, and then the sock, while Jorkens sat in his chair quietly drinking one of my whiskeys.

Terbut looked all over the foot, and so did we all, and certainly there was neither scar nor scratch.

We were silent till Terbut spoke. I, for one, could make nothing of it. And then Terbut said: "Not a sign of one."

"That's because you're looking at the wrong foot," said Jorkens, glancing up from his whiskey.

You wouldn't think that would have ended it, but it did. Terbut looked thoroughly fooled. And, strange as it may appear, not one of us asked to look at the other foot. Then Jorkens, rapping down the empty glass on the table, walked out of the club with an air.

In the Garden of Memories

I never heard the beginning of this story. I never heard exactly how it happened, and Jorkens never referred to it again. Jorkens was already talking as I came into the Club. And I saw by his look, so far from us and the club, and the world as it lies today outside our window, that he told of the long past. "I must have seen the house many times," he was saying, "before I knew that it was there. I must have often looked straight at it from far off and seen its whitish wall among the trees, and the dark roof above it; but the roof was so like the dark mass of the trees, and the wall so like the glare of a grey sky, that I never knew I was looking at the house. As you came near it, it was completely hidden by the high wall of the garden. Sometimes I wondered what was behind the garden wall, but the ivy on top of it seemed to hide it all with a frown, and though my wonder found out more than my eyes, which as yet had made out nothing, I got no further than guesses till the day that I shot the snipe, and it went away about three hundred yards, then soared and suddenly dropped; and that led me up to the wall, but there was no gate. When I could find no entrance of any sort I put down my gun and tried to climb at the lowest part of the wall, but I found as soon as I put my hand upon it that the old wall that had crumbled already, crumbled faster under my hand than it had done under the years. The mortar was only dust: it seemed only waiting for the touch of a hand, but none ever came. And now the grey stones fell so easily from their places that soon I was on the top without far to climb, and more stones slid away as I dropped on the other side. There lay before me a garden beside a river, the house at the far end of the garden. The house was in the middle of the far wall, and on the side of the river there was no wall at all, the water giving there the seclusion in which the old house seemed to have wrapped itself. Even where I stood I was not quite in the garden, but amongst a group of trees sheltered by two walls; between me and the garden a stream ran down to the river. The stream, at any rate in its last few yards, was a bit too broad for jumping, but a strange old arch of stone led over it to the garden. No track whatever led over the little bridge.

"I stood a long while there, looking into the garden. My snipe must have fallen into the river, and would soon come drifting past, but still I stood there gazing. It is hard to say what I was looking at; a few shrubs, something that looked like a path going up the middle, and a man alone, bent over a trowel, seeming to be doing some work in face of the contempt of triumphant weeds, and the old house all silent beyond him. It was nothing that I saw that gripped me there. But never have I known any place that called up such hosts of memories. They surged down the path, they rioted through the shrubs, the very air was enchanted with them, and the river going by like Beethoven seemed to be awed and hushed by them."

I never quite understood what Jorkens meant by the river going by like Beethoven, I asked him once, and he said "Oh, the sixth symphony." But he never explained why.

"They were not my memories. I knew nothing of the place. They were the garden's memories."

"The garden's memories?" asked someone, a little puzzled, though not doubting Jorkens.

"I don't know what it was," said Jorkens. "I don't know if they were always there, or if they came once every hundred years, or when they came; but they were there then. They were there in masses, un-mistakable memories, of days long past. They had such a hold on that garden, that I saw it first confused between the two visions; the garden as it then was, with the man in his shirt-sleeves dully bent over the trowel, doing work that seemed almost hopeless against the huge weeds; and the garden as it lived in its own memories, sometimes nick-ering faint, so that you saw the weeds through the lawns, sometimes flaring so strong that you saw nothing but the lilac in bloom and the three girls walking down trim paths through the flowers. Yes, there were three girls there, I could tell you the colour of their dresses, I could even describe their features. One was dressed in green, another in lilac, and the third in yellow.

They were dark, and all the three were young. At first I could not focus them: I saw the two scenes overlapping. But very soon I saw nothing except the memory. I saw the house bright, and flashing back the sunlight; I saw the woodwork of the windows freshly painted a clear green; I saw curtains trimly tied, behind the windows; I saw win-ter gone and the lilac all in bloom, and the garden full of arbours and little paths, and neat green lawns wherever the flower-beds ended.

"You saw them?" said Terbut.

"I imagined them," replied Jorkens. "But so vividly that, except when the memories faded a little, as they did every now and then, I could see nothing else for the strength of them. It was a matter of focus. As a louder sound can drown a weaker one, so these memories overcame the weeds and the desolation. I take it that the strength of the memories, that were more abundant in that deserted garden than in any other place I have ever seen, so dominated the imagination of anybody that ever chanced to come there that it became impossible, standing just where I stood, and with nothing else to distract me, to see anything else with any clearness at all. That's how I look at it now; but at the time, so clear were those young faces, so bright the sunlight on those silken dresses, so sweet and heavy the lilac, that only their momentary fading, as the memories seemed to wane, assured me that they were not living beside me, and even then I could not believe that they haunted the garden from any distance away; so that I crossed the little stone bridge and went to the man digging, and first of all apologized for having broken the wall. As I entered the garden over the tributary of the river, the lilac faded, February returned, and the girls on the garden paths went with the lilac. To my apology for the wall the man with the trowel answered listlessly, as he turned to me, 'Oh, it's always falling.' Then I told him that I wished to call on the ladies that lived in that house, that I was sure I had known them, though a long time ago, and that I had not been able to find the way up to the house, or any door in the wall. And he said that nobody lived there.

"Well, he was there: he was a live man working in the garden. And so I told him. If he wasn't the gardener, who was? And what was he?

"And he said that he had been given the right to plant a few vegetables there, and no one lived in the house. He didn't seem to mind my having doubted him, any more than he minded the knocking down of the stones where I climbed in over the wall; the queerness of the place, and the lapse of time over its weeds and wall, he seemed to take for granted as much as he did the floating by of the river. But to quiet my doubt for ever he led me by a track, that was probably his alone, through the weedy tangle by which he planted his vegetables, to the old door of the house, looking first at the fallen stones that I had upset in my climb, as though he would put them back, but seeming to change his mind, if he ever had made it up, and deciding to let them lie.

"Till the gardener opened the door I hoped yet to see those young and beautiful ladies, whose memory so haunted the garden that I could not believe they were far from me either in time or space. When the door opened I saw at once that they were only dreams and imaginings.

Nobody dwelt there, no one had done so for ages. The door opened on to a darkness that showed at once that the spider lived there doing his work in the quiet, and that nothing was there but dust and the passing of years. That was the feel of it the moment I entered, and I might have guessed it from the look of the door. For the door was not only cracked, and slightly sagging, and decayed where the damp splashed up on rainy days from below, but it was that strange greeny blue that paint goes after a long time, paint that was once probably green, but a colour now that is never painted on anything; and flakes of the paint were curling away from the wood. A dampness blew at me as I went inside; and something else was there as strong as the damp, a feeling that I intruded upon the hush and the echoes, trespassing on the state kept there in the calm by the spider. It was that feeling, as much as the damp and the rust, that assured me that no one dwelt there; though it was evident enough from the great festoons of the spider, without any of the subtler perceptions, that the upholstering and the tending of these dim chambers was done no more by man. There is something that man sets up between himself and the wild, an air that there is in all inhabited houses, that sets them unmistakably apart from mere patches of untamed land or from any shelter in which wild animals hide; it is a certain feeling that goes with the word indoors, being made of comfort and of things familiar and orderly, and has nothing to do with moonlight or cries of owls hunting, or breezes that whisper at night under leaves and round trunks and through grasses. This feeling was wholly gone. I had not the sense of being indoors at all. Whatever barriers there be between us and the wild, in the desolate house they were down. There was no need to stand any longer inside the half-opened door where the gardener had pushed it as far as he could, along the mould and the grit, over which it had grated, hanging heavily on its hinges; no need to gather evidence that what he had said was right: nobody dwelt here.

"'Yes,' I said, 'they are gone.' And I turned away. As I spoke I saw a look in the face of the gardener, but for which I would have asked him of those three girls. But his face went blank as I spoke, blank as the garden bleak with weeds and all empty of flowers, and I somehow saw that I should get no more news from him of those gracious girls that dwelt there once, as I knew, than I should find trace of their feet on those paths, if paths you could call the narrow strips along which he walked through the weeds. And so I turned away.

"Once more I apologized before I went; but I saw, as I spoke, that no one from outside that garden could hold his attention for long, and the fall of the bit of the wall was clearly too much in keeping with the age-old decay all around him for him to think of it twice. Half way down the ruined garden he came with me; but, when he reached the spot at which I had found him digging, he returned to his lonely work. And all the way past the arbours and over the lawns, as they had appeared to me once, I saw that these things were only patches of dock-weed, and wandering weeds and tall teasel, with the brown stalks of convolvulus running wild through them all. And yet when I crossed the little bridge and looked back again through the trees, even once again the memories swept up, and rode down Time; and once again I saw the lawns and the arbours, the lilac flickering into bloom and fading again, and then triumphantly blooming, and the three girls once again flashing by on the paths, appearing and disappearing amongst tall shrubs blooming in splendour.

"The gardener was wholly sunk in his work again, his back to me and his face to the earth; so for a little while yet I stood and watched the garden, wondering whether the force of those memories had been so rare that it had stamped them upon the world for ever, or whether in the damp of that secluded place, cut off by wall and river from Time's interference, the mild air had some peculiar effect upon memories, causing them to luxuriate as the seeds of flowers flourish in certain soils. Whichever it was I supposed that the imagination of anybody coming among those memories would be enormously stimulated, and that it would see according to its power. As I looked at the gardener bowed down over what must have been his vegetables, in the midst of all that neat beauty preserved from the loot of the years, I do admit I compared my own power to see with the dull blindness of his imagination. Well, well, we all flatter ourselves.

"I looked to the river then, to see about my snipe. It had long drifted by. So I turned to my gap in the wall, to leave the garden. And even as I turned I saw them again, their faces seeming all the lovelier for the distance I knew them to be from me, remote beyond hope. For all I knew their graves might be deeper in weeds than that garden. But they were coming towards me now, coming straight past the gardener, down one of those little paths; he was working within two yards of it. Could they mean nothing to him? Could he who knew that garden so well, working alone there, see nothing of what my imagination showed me so clearly? His face was still to the earth, and they drew nearer and nearer. I turned to go. I wished to carry away the memory with me before that attitude of his overcame it, disenchanting the garden and leaving me with mere facts and the sagging weeds. Already the focus of the imagined garden was trembling, as though about to fade and to let the dock-leaves through. Now the three girls seemed level with the gardener, whose face was still to the earth. I would have gone then, but I saw him sigh. Then he lifted his head as they passed, and touched his cap, and went on with his digging.

"I saw it now: I was tired after my day's shooting in those long marshes, and my imagination was weak; I could imagine those lonely figures a little while, then they faded away and the lilac flickered back into winter; but he could see them. I left the garden then, and glancing round as I left I saw the river. It seemed to be going by like triumphant Time."

The Slugly Beast

Of all the remarkable things that I have ever heard Jorkens say, it is odd that the most remarkable should have been not of times long since, but of only last year, and that I should have been able to check it and, to some extent, to be even a witness of the strange adventure that followed.

Some of us at the Club were talking of wireless, when somebody said that on his wireless set he had once got a bit of a programme from Auckland in New Zealand. I forget what our comments were, but I shall never forget the quiet remark of Jorkens, when the rest of us had all finished. "They go further than that," he said.

A few disagreed with Jorkens, and the talk drifted away, but I sat silent, overwhelmed by the wonder of what Jorkens had said. And after a while, when the others were talking among themselves, I said to Jorkens, "Further?" And he nodded his head. No more than that did I say, but when Jorkens rose to go I went away with him, and outside in the street I said: "What was that message?"

"It's only a few words," said Jorkens. "It's all they can get."

"Where is it?" I asked.

"Terner's got it," said Jorkens.

"From?" I said.

"Mars," said he.

I called a taxi and Jorkens got in. "The old address?" I said, and he nodded, and soon we were going towards that rather dingy room beyond Charing Cross Road, in which Terner had told me once of his journey to Mars, and of the lovely girl he met there, a tale which, owing to his own fault in bringing back no convincing proofs, the public had so thoroughly disbelieved. Whether publication of his story in the Saturday Evening Post has caused them to alter their verdict I cannot know for certain, though some letters I have received partly lead me to hope so. Let it suffice that this disbelief had so much embittered Terner that he is little likely to have been affected by any reparation that may have come later. On the way from the club to Terner's rooms Jorkens told me that, as is often the case with men who are deeply interested in anything, he refused to see any impossibility, any improbability even, in the thing that he longed for happening. What Terner had longed for, for the last seven years, was a message from the girl he had left in Mars. That the people in Mars were more refined, more highly civilized than ours, he had seen at a glance; deducing from that that anything we understood, they knew far more of, he argued, as love will, that some communication with his lost lady was possible. He seemed to have overlooked the point that a race greatly superior to man in power, though fouler than any beast on our planet, which held man under lock and key in Mars, as Terner had seen, was not likely to allow him to send out any messages for help to Earth, where man, as this beast probably knew, was free. And yet Terner hoped, and had done little else for the last seven years. "And the message?" I said. But we were at Terner's door now.

And there was Terner, much the same as ever; older, but still smoking cigarettes, and with his thoughts still far from our planet. He remembered me, and I got his attention at once, by reminding him how he had shot the loathsome beast in Mars, that had just wrung the necks of a boy and a girl that it kept in a sort of chicken-run, and by letting him see that I wholly believed his story. Then he talked. He talked almost as though he were continuing the story that he had told me two or three years ago, almost as though we had never gone out of the room. He had been watching wireless for years. He had several sets: he seemed to have bought a new one whenever he could afford it. But the strange thing about him and his wireless was, that while we listen to music or the accounts of baseball matches, or whatever we do listen to, and sometimes impatiently curse atmospherics, or whatever those noisy interruptions are, he listened only to atmospherics. Those shrill hoots that we sometimes hear, or those deep buzzing noises that utterly ruin a song, to him were the only things of any interest whatever. And gradually from amongst them he picked out some, that at first had clearly no connection with any known broadcasting station, or any meaning whatever, and then began to have resemblances to a certain type that he came to know, and from that became definite messages, which he at last decoded.

"But in what language?" I said.

"In English," he answered. "Yes, they must have been getting our broadcasts for years, especially I think Daventry, and I take it they worked out our language. Probably it seemed quite simple to them, though I don't know how they did it. I have pages covered with scraps of messages that I employed to decode the kind of noisy Morse that they use. Whom they were to, or what they were about, I don't know; but, do you know, the very first message that I was able to make out was a message to me."

"To you!" I exclaimed.

"To myself," he repeated. "It was simply addressed to The Airman from Earth. There are people who won't believe that I ever went there; but certainly nobody else did. It could have been meant for nobody else. There it is."

"A loving message from Mars," I blurted out in my astonishment.

"Not very," he said.

And then I read it. And these are the words exactly. "The slugly beast is waiting for you."

That it wasn't quite English did not surprise me; what surprised me was that six words out of the seven were perfect English, and whenever I think it over another thing surprises me more, and that is the vividly horrible picture that the one word that wasn't English at all conjured up in my mind. And the more I reflected on the unreasonableness of this, the more loathsomely crawled in my imagination the vile form of the slugly beast.

I read it over two or three times.

Then I said to Terner: "Something foul, isn't it?"

Terner nodded his head.

"A friend of the thing you shot?" I asked.

"Must be," said Terner; "or why trouble to send me this?"

Horrible pictures crossed my mind as I thought on a situation that I had never dreamed of before.

"What will you do?" I asked.

And a light shone in his eyes, and brightened all his face. "I am going back," he said.

This was only last year and Mars was again at his nearest, after those journeys of him and us through Space, that had kept us apart for nearly seven years.

"When?" I asked.

"It's a dead secret," he said. "If they knew where I was going they would think me mad, and not let me go up. They believe nothing."

"I won't tell a soul," I said.

I saw that Jorkens knew. Terner looked at him as though to ask if he thought that I could be trusted. Jorkens nodded.

"Tomorrow night," said Terner.

"Tomorrow night!" I exclaimed, the nearness of it making me wonder more at the whole adventure than I had done already.

"Yes," said Terner.

It's a curious thing, but I don't believe that even love would have made Terner take that journey. Jorkens never thought so either. That he was in love with the girl that he left in Mars there is no doubt whatever, though she may have been killed and eaten long ago; but I don't believe that he would ever have gone there again if it had not been for the message, fury alone leading him to that stupendous adventure to which nothing else would have lured him.

"What weapons will you take?" I asked him.

"Revolvers," he said, "and a very light machine gun; and soft-nosed bullets for all of them."

Something in the gusto with which he spoke of soft-nosed bullets made me quite sure he would go.

"He has a good deal to arrange," said Jorkens. For he had seen, though I never noticed it, that Terner wished to be alone. And then we left, but not until I had got Terner's permission to come down to Ketling aerodrome and see him off on his journey on the following night. The street looked all new and strange to me when we got outside, so absorbed was I with the vastness of Terner's adventure, and so unable to notice most of the things that made up the street I knew; or was it that my imagination, over-stimulated by the mere fact of meeting Terner, saw scores of things in that street that my duller wits had never seen before? I don't know which it was, but the street looked brighter and wider, and full of odd details. Terner had got the message some weeks ago, Jorkens told me as we walked away, and had been working on his aeroplane ever since, and filling in forms about his weapons and ammunition.

"That didn't take him long; did it?" I asked.

"Well, you see," said Jorkens, "they asked him what he wanted all that ammunition for, and he said for rhinoceros, thinking that that would just satisfy them. Unfortunately the man he was talking to knew something of Africa, and he said, 'You don't want soft-nosed bullets for rhinos.' And Terner had to start all over again. And he hadn't much time; he had to attend to his aeroplane."

"What's he doing on that?" I asked.

"He has the old rocket-attachment," he said, "to increase his speed enough to get clear of the pull of Earth. Once outside that his motive power will be what it was before, the pace with which we are all moving, the pace of Earth round the sun. That will take him to Mars."

"Yes, he told me," I said.

"But what is quite new," said Jorkens, "is his protection against space. Nothing he used last time seemed adequate to him. So this time he is to be entirely shut in by a tiny cabin; he will have his supply of compressed air there, and the walls of it are capable of resisting the emptiness of Space. He will be much more comfortable that way."

"And when," I asked with an uneasy feeling, "when is he coming back?"

"That," said Jorkens, "is the difficulty."

"Will he manage it?" I said. "It was a near thing last time."

"He wants to get this beast first," said Jorkens "and as many of them as possible. It is disgusting that it should be alive at all, eating man." And Jorkens spat. I have seldom seen him so moved. "But the trouble is," he continued, "that he can't stay there more than five weeks, or he'll never get home at all."

"Mars will be getting away from us," I said.

"And it isn't only that," said Jorkens. "You see he's got an idea that at his age and with his physique the time he can live in rarefied air is limited. Yes, it's rarefied there, a rather smaller planet; less air on it. And he's been to a heart specialist, and talked to him all about it. It must have been a curious conversation, for though he told him all about the air there, and just how it affected his breathing, he never told him he'd been to Mars."

"Never told him?" I said.

"No," said Jorkens. "He said these specialists were all in together. So he said he had been living on a high table-land, I think he said in East Africa, and told him he was soon going back, and how would he stand it? The difficulty was the doctor kept asking him how many feet above sea-level, and Terner could only say he didn't know; but he described the feel of the air pretty well, and the specialist pounded his heart, and what Terner arrived at in the end was that five to ten weeks would be about his limit. You see he couldn't live in the aeroplane, breathing his compressed air, because he wanted that for his return journey."

"Heart bad?" I asked.

"No," said Jorkens, "but you can't go to certain altitudes after a certain age, so they say. And the air of Mars seems to be like what we keep on our highest mountain tops."

We were walking back to the club, and now we arrived there, and we went in and talked of Terner, all alone at the time when no one is there, between lunch and dinner. We neither of us dined there that night, we fixed on a train to take us to Ketling next day, and I went to bed early. All night my mind was full, and my dreams troubled, with hideous pictures of the slugly beast.

Well, next day Jorkens and I met at Waterloo Station, and went down to Ketling together in the afternoon. Was it possible to dissuade him, I asked Jorkens. And Jorkens said: "Quite impossible."

After that we talked little: I for one was too full of uneasy apprehensions.

At Ketling there was Terner, dressed for his journey, and walking about smoking.

"When?" I asked him.

"When Mars rises," he said.

Jorkens talked alone with him then, but, whatever final arrangements they were making, dissuasion was evidently out of the question. Presently a mechanic came up and interrupted them, and I rejoined them then, just as the mechanic said: "Where are you off to, sir?" And I heard Terner say: "I'm going to investigate the composition of the upper air-currents."

And I saw that he had learned to talk nonsense, where truth would have been taken for craziness, which is one of the things that the cleverest men never learn.

And then he turned, and began talking earnestly to Jorkens again. And this time I heard what he was talking about: it was all about his bullets. "At the tip," he was saying, "I have the softest lead that is made, and of course quite hollow. The beasts are all soft themselves; those expanding bullets will play hell with them."

I didn't especially disapprove of this gloating, at least not to the extent of showing disapproval in my face; and yet he must have seen some such expression on me, for he turned to me and said quietly: "You haven't seen these beasts. And you haven't seen the way they treat men."

He was perfectly right, and I told him so.

And evening wore away, and we had a brief meal together in an inn that there was a little way from the aerodrome. There was a good deal of silence at that supper, and a drink or two to the dim future, without much said. When we came out it was night. A few last preparations by Terner, and then all three of us were standing silent, watching the line of the hills. And over the hills came the enemy.

You've all seen Mars rise, so there's little to tell you, except that he was larger than he usually is, and except that we probably looked at him with different feelings from the feelings with which any other three men had ever watched him before. Only Terner seemed to be regarding him calmly.

And then Terner got into his plane which was there on the landing ground all ready for him, with its head pointing straight to the ruddy light of Mars, like a huge moth eyeing a flame. And we shut the door that was to remain shut on him for a month in that cramped enclosure. Then they started his propeller and the thing ran forward roaring, and lifted and was off to the red star.

He should have had lights, and as only he knew how useless they would be he must have had some difficulty in leaving Ketling without them, but he certainly had none, so that soon we lost the dark bulk of the aeroplane in the night. But before we quite lost the roar of it we heard it curving round to the left and coming back towards us, and very soon it was down again on the landing-ground. We ran up and asked what he wanted, and he showed by signs through the thick glass that he wished to correct his aim. I often wondered if that was really the reason, or if what Terner wanted was to have one more look at Earth. Whatever it was, he was off again almost at once, and this time sight and sound of his plane were soon lost to us, as we stood there gazing towards Mars. For nearly ten minutes we stood there without moving, gazing at the star that seemed crouching over the hills. Mechanics began to look curiously at us. And then, as small as a star, yet wonderfully clear, the brightest speck of colour among a million lights, the first of Terner's rockets shone out to the right of Mars. Another and then another, gaudily trespassing on the calm of the night. He was gaining the speed that before he left our air was to wrench him free of the ancient course of Earth; for he was aiming a little wider than our orbit, on such a bearing that, hurled through space by the force of Earth's journey, he would meet Mars travelling outside us. In the same way when Earth got ahead, as she would in a few weeks, he meant to return, hurled back by the pace of Mars. But to break free from the ancient journey of either Earth or Mars he needed the power of an enormous speed, to gain which he was firing rockets. When the rockets ceased we knew he was nearing Earth's outermost limit, that boundary-fence of thin air on the other side of which lies nothing whatever. And then after the last of the rockets, a single gay green light fell from the direction that Terner had taken, floating downward as slowly as though it scorned gravity. It was Terner's farewell to our planet.

A month to go, a month to return, and five weeks there, gave us the date by which he must be back if we were ever to see him again. It had not needed Jorkens' or my advice to urge him to bring back copious and incontrovertible proofs of his journey to Mars this time. He was not going to be doubted again. Meanwhile he had told nobody but us two. And both of us kept his secret.

We went seldom to the club; I think Jorkens felt as I did, that there was only one thing worth talking about, and that was a secret from everybody except each other. So we only talked to each other. I saw a lot of Jorkens in those days. At first we were full of plans as to how Terner was to be introduced to the world. We came to realize that to bring him before great audiences in London, New York and Paris would be little better than hiding him in a village. The whole world would want to see him. Oh, the plans we made. But as the weeks wore on we spoke less and less of what Terner was to do in Tokio, Delhi or Brussels, and more of the probable outcome of his encounter with the slugly beast, as it called itself. I often told Jorkens, we often told each other, that there was no need for anxiety until the very last day, because he was certain to stay till the very last in order to gratify as widely as possible the quiet calm loathing that he felt for these foul things that had challenged him.

And then the day arrived, a huge red sunset and the air full of the threat of winter. We both of us telephoned frequently to Ketling, wrapping up our enquiries for Terner as well as we could, without any hint of Mars. Ketling knew nothing of him. I don't think I spoke to anyone except Jorkens next day. There was just the chance of his having landed on some distant part of our planet, but when no news whatever came of any such airman in any part of our world we gave up hope in a week.

Jorkens and I still met and talked alone. Every evening in his rooms we used to sit and talk about Terner till midnight or the small hours. And gradually as we talked we put together a theory that those soft flabby beasts, so vulnerable to bullets, must have got some deadly weapon or other means of destruction, before they sent that provocative message to Terner. Piecing together everything we knew about Terner, and everything he had told us of Mars, the state of his health, the rarity of the air, the powers and appetites of those revolting creatures, and working out the details of what had happened like two men analyzing a game of chess, or planning a campaign, we came to decide that Terner must have been overpowered by numbers, and prevented by something of which neither he nor we could know anything from using his machine-gun and pistols with their hollow-pointed bullets. And now that Mars had passed out of reach of Earth, to be gone apart from us for another seven years, we assumed that Terner was dead, an assumption for which we obtained legal sanction without any mention of Mars. And there was a memorial service for him in London, which many airmen attended, for he had credit at least for the flights that he had made on this earth. All that was known to the clergyman who preached briefly on this occasion, all that was known to anyone but Jorkens and me, was that Terner had left the aerodrome at night, and his end had its place with the fates of those who had been swallowed up in mystery. The clergyman spoke awhile of the vivid present, and then of the mystery that surrounds all of us. Jorkens and I of course were there, and we each left a wreath that day at his old rooms near Charing Cross Road, and the old charwoman that tidied the rooms had left a bunch of flowers there in a glass on his table, which I felt was the last farewell that the world took of Terner.

And then next day there came a message in plain Morse from an unknown station, a message followed by Terner's initials, A.V.T.: several stations got it and many private sets, and no one knew where it came from: and Jorkens got it on Terner's own set that he had kept for him all those weeks, fixed at a certain wave-length that Terner had given him, and with the stop out night and day. It said: "Victory. Victory. Victory."

Earth's Secret

We had a talk, one day at the club, of a highly scientific nature. Such a talk may be interesting, and certainly instructive, if there is only one scientist talking. He has to make himself clear to the rest. But on this day there were two of them. That may appear to have made it twice as interesting: as a matter of fact it was the dullest talk I have heard in the club for a long time. You see, they each knew what the other was talking about, so that there was no necessity to make themselves any clearer. And being on their own subject they soon got very keen, and there was no stopping them. It was all very tedious. They were on the age-old theme of the alchemists, but were giving modern and very learned reasons why the dream of the alchemists was impossible. Base metals, they were saying, could never be turned into gold; but I have said that their talk was tedious, bad enough for us in the club where we couldn't escape it, but unthinkable for my reader, who can fly from such things by a mere flick of the page. So I will tell the tale from the moment at which any brightness came into it, any merriment, any audacity; and not, I hope, without some advantage to science. It was when Jorkens spoke, on top of their weighty reasons against the making of gold. "I made some once," he said.

"You made some?" they said together.

"A small pot-full," said Jorkens.

Then we all asked him how it was, and so we got his story.

"Some while ago, in Asia, far up a mountain," said Jorkens, "a man was living alone, higher up than the monkeys, and higher than all the villages. And when I came once in my travels to his curious pagoda-like house . . ."

"Where was it?" asked Terbut.

"He made me swear not to reveal it," Jorkens answered; "but the oath was not very binding, on account of his having sworn me by gods for whom I have little respect, disgusting gods really; the things they used to do, and take a delight in doing, if the tales about them were true! The things people sang about them! Well, let's forget them. The oath can't have been binding. It isn't that that stops me from telling you. But the world, you know, is contracting a bit as it cools; little enough if you take the whole bulk of it, but it plays the devil with the crust; wrinkles it, bores holes in it, and one thing and another. You know they've got a theory that the Andes are moving slightly, away from the Himalayas, and that that is the cause latterly of a good deal of the subsidence and upheavals that has been recorded on seismographs."

"Are we going to have some more science?" said Terbut.

And I admit that he voiced the apprehensions of most of us.

"Briefly," said Jorkens, "that mountain is now a volcano."

"Oh," said Terbut, and was silent; for he was not the intrepid traveller that Jorkens was.

"But in those days," Jorkens continued, "it was a snow-capped mountain, with the man I was telling you of living just at the edge of the snow, bits of it running along ravines far under him, and his goats wandering about, which, with a few lean-looking chickens, seemed all that he had for sustenance, besides a very small patch of cabbages, and the mountain streams. There he lived and grew a narrow and very long beard, and I suppose meditated. I was able to do him a small service, in exchange for which he gave me a kind of little note-book of thin leaves covered with figures. It was in fact the secret of making gold."

"A small service?" said Terbut.

"Well," said Jorkens, "it was easily done."

"And he gave you the secret of gold for it?"

"Yes, certainly," replied Jorkens. But we could all see that he was getting embarrassed.

"You must have been of great service to him," said Terbut.

"No, no," said Jorkens, "it was nothing much. Not at all."

We have not often seen Jorkens embarrassed, and the hunting sense in Terbut, if you can call it by any so sporting a name, was much excited by it; so that he soon got out of Jorkens what that small service had been. He wavered for a moment between bare truth and his amour propre, and then blurted out the bare truth.

"He told me," said Jorkens, "that he was bound by his religion to give me food and shelter, but that, if I would go at once without demanding his hospitality, he would give me the secret of gold. Evidently not a very friendly fellow. No herd instinct, I mean. And giving me the secret of gold meant nothing to the contrary, because I could see by his face as he gave me the little bundle of pages that he regarded it as the root of all evil; a kind of contemptuous look as he gave me the secret. And another thing that I didn't like about the fellow was the serenity that seemed to come on his face when I accepted his book and left, a nasty sort of calm and a glow in his eyes. But never mind that;

I knew I had the best of the bargain; and, if he didn't like me, I didn't like his long thin dark beard, going grey at the edges, or the way he lived, or dressed, or anything whatever about him. Who ever heard of green silk up a mountain! Yet, whatever rot his meditations were, or his philosophy and all that, his recipe for the making of gold was perfectly sound. I didn't know much Tibetan, the language in which he wrote it, and I had to get it translated bit by bit so as not to awake suspicions, which took a long time, but I soon saw what he was driving at; the main idea was simple enough; it was merely that to make an element you need all the other elements. There are about forty of them; take away one, and the remainder all together will make up the missing one. I believe a similar law holds good with colours. But it wasn't anything like as easy as it may sound, because all these elements had to be blended in the most exact proportions, according to their various weights, so that the total weight of all of them should be precisely the weight of the same bulk of gold; without that, I was warned, the experiment would be not only useless but dangerous. And the calculation of all those weights was, as you may suppose, intensely elaborate. That's what the book was about.

"Well, as soon as I got to understand the book, and to understand the queer names he had for the elements, it was easy to follow the figures, their numerals being no harder to read than ours. So that it was not necessary for me to take the tedious and dangerous course of making a copy in English, dangerous not only because there is twice as much risk of theft when you have two copies, but because an English copy could be so readily understood by anybody who stole it. I didn't want another man going about making gold; it would have cut prices.

"Well, I got out of that country as soon as I had the thing clear; and I got it clear without any native suspecting what the scraps and lines he translated could be about; and that wasn't too easy, for they begin on suspicion before you've started to talk to them, and they are all of them pretty neat in following it up.

"I never had the papers out of my reach until I got to London; in my pocket or under my pillow, night and day. It was a packet of eighty pages or so, very thin paper, about four inches by three, just like a little note-book without a cover. I met no one with whom I'd have trusted it, till I got home, as I used to call the lodgings I had down Wimbledon way. And there was my old landlady in the doorway as I came up the path. She was delighted to see me back, if I may say so, though it could only have been the reflection of my pleasure at seeing her, for what had I ever done for Mrs. Mergins? Whereas she had brought comfort into my life whenever I was in England. She was a very soothing influence in the house; more than that; from her there seemed to radiate an orderliness and a quiet, which but for her would have been replaced by litter and a perpetual searching for papers. A woman with a quiet face, going grey. I had been her first lodger and she had asked me to name her house for her, because she didn't like a mere number. There was some opposition at first to the name I chose, even criticism, among the neighbours near Wimbledon; but it was no affair of theirs; and she seemed to me so perfect a landlady, so truly the very type of our English lodging-house-keeper, that I could think of no other name. I called it Sea View.

"With the details of the furniture of Sea View I shall not trouble you. You have probably seen plenty like it. For myself I think it is a beautiful thing that there should be people, after all these years, really to love plush. But there is one detail I must refer to, a silver bowl I once won in a quarter mile. Yes, a quarter mile, and I was a light-weight too. It was the size of a good large sugar-basin, and Mrs. Mergins kept it as Elaine kept the shield of Lancelot, or whoever did keep it; I'm not very strong on myth, though it's better than history."

"Better? Why?" I asked.

"No dates in it," replied Jorkens. "Well this bowl was kept as silver ought to be kept, except that it was cleaned far too often. Always bright, always shining, whether I was at home or not, it stood always on the same table, giving a certain air to the room; and never dinted or scratched since Mrs. Mergins first handled it. So that when I entered Sea View and saw Mrs. Mergins and gave her that little bundle of thin Tibetan paper, the first person with whom I would trust it after coming eight thousand miles, the actual words I used, and they are important, were: 'Keep it as you keep my silver bowl. It is much more valuable.' Those were my exact words, and I couldn't have made them stronger, because the value that Mrs. Mergins had chosen to place on my bowl was beyond all reason, as the care that she took of it was beyond praise.

"Well, I hadn't been home many days when I had all the elements bought, and soon I was tediously weighing them out in their exact proportions. I remember the day I put them all into the saucepan and lit an enormous fire, and handed back the papers into Mrs. Mergins' safe keeping. The work before me, the melting down of a pound of mixed metals, was nothing, compared with the calculations of days and days, with the Tibetan figures beside me on the table, opposite the minutest scales, in which I weighed everything to the fractions of grammes. When that quiet work was over, the active work with the roaring fire and the bellows, however uncomfortable, seemed to me like a holiday. My mind was muzzy with those calculations, and somehow the blazing heat on my face seemed rather to clear it than otherwise. You've no idea of the thousands of figures that I had had to plod through. But never mind that now; the results of those calculations were all in the pot, and the pot was gradually glowing. My eyes were sore, my face was dripping, my fingers were actually burnt, and still the metals in the pot, though turning white, remained solid. I had made the room like a stoke-hole. And all of a sudden the metals collapsed and ran into liquid. It happened so swiftly that I had no receptacle ready. I couldn't keep the gold in the saucepan: Mrs. Mergins would want it for cooking. I looked round, holding the handle with a duster, and my hand burning through that, and my eye fell on the bowl; Mrs. Mergins' beloved object, my silver bowl. I knew that the molten mass was sure to spoil it, but I think I was rather amused by the idea of spoiling a thin piece of silver with solid gold. I wondered what Mrs. Mergins would say when she saw what it was that had tarnished it. And I was wondering how much longer I should be able to hold that handle before the duster caught fire. So I went as fast as I could to the silver bowl, which shone in the dimness caused by my half-boiled eyes, and poured the metal in. A puff of smoke went up like a tiny explosion, and under it lay my metal, half filling the bowl: it turned red, and cooled, and was yellow; and I saw that I had made gold."

"And was it gold?" said Terbut.

"Certainly," answered Jorkens, "a pound weight of it."

"Did you go on making it?" asked Terbut.

Jorkens rubbed his chin.

"It was exactly what I meant to do," said Jorkens. "I took a few hours rest before going back to that awful work on the figures; and then I went to my landlady and said: 'Where are the papers?' That was the way I put it this time, though I usually asked her to be so kind as to get them. I don't know what impulse it was that made me say 'Where are the papers?' And she said: 'In the silver bowl.'

"I could only say 'What,' and she repeated it, and added, 'Where you told me to put them.'

"Of course I'd never . . . Oh well. Waiter!"

There are times when Jorkens, for all the brilliancy of his memory, deliberately forgets the past.

The Persian Spell

"I told you of my lodgings near Wimbledon," said Jorkens one day, "Richmond as a matter of fact. Kept by a Mrs. Mergins."

He began thus after lunch, gazing up into the past, not started off by anything we had said, indeed no one was talking at all when he began. Something seemed to have brought the past somehow all round him, and he was gazing into it and talking as he gazed. He may have been a bit oblivious of us, and I would not at that moment have asked him any of those trifles of our present day upon which one asks advice at a club, such as the effect of the colour of buses upon their destination; but I am sure that he was not inventing. He was seeing the past again, and telling us what he saw. What does it matter how he came to see it?

"She'd a bit of a kitchen garden at the back," he went on; "little wooden palings dividing it from the gardens on either side, but at the end of it ran the great wall of Richmond park. I was sitting there one evening in the summer. It is wonderful how secluded you can often be, within nine miles of Charing Cross. There was hardly a sound to hear besides birds singing, and the wind in the tops of the trees on the other side of the wall. I had lit my pipe and was thinking about things; not so much of things that I had actually known, as the things that with a bit of luck might have easily come my way; well they never did in the end, but they might have then, and there was no harm in thinking them over as I sat there smoking my pipe; I should have been all the readier to make the most of them when they arrived, for having thought them over a bit."

"What sort of things were you expecting?" asked Terbut.

But Jorkens never heard him speak, and went straight on with his story, gazing beyond us to the darkened end of the room, for a winter's evening was already upon us. "And then a very curious thing occurred. I was gazing at the wall, and the long arms of a plum-tree that was growing against it, when I began to notice that there was a man climbing quietly down the plum-tree, stepping from branch to branch. So softly was he coming that one did not notice at first, in the fading light of the evening, that he was really there. And then the unusualness of his method of entering the garden suddenly caught my attention. And yet the moment he began to speak, all idea of anything unusual about him vanished. It's curious that: there are men that awaken your doubts if you see them on your front door-step, with a card in their hand, just waiting for someone to open the door; while another will come down your chimney and seem just the man you'd expect, and on a perfectly plausible errand. It's the second kind you should usually mistrust; but no one ever does.

"What was I saying? Yes, a man climbing down the plum-tree, late in the evening. He said, 'I was afraid that, if I called earlier, I might not find you in.'

"'Well, I am out in the garden,' I answered.

"'An excellent place for a quiet talk,' he replied.

"And mind you, I had never met the man before.

"'You come from . . .' I began, trying to make out which neighbour he was, of the thousands that surrounded one there.

"'From home,' he answered.

"And something in the way he said it made me say: 'You don't mean The Home?'

"'Yes,' he replied.

"Well that's the name we had for the looney house, a nice quiet villa a mile away, with a tennis court that you see from the road.

"'You're on the staff there?' I said by way of politeness.

"'I escaped,' he answered. And then he added, it was really very nice of him, 'If you find anything whatever in my conduct, or even my manner, in any way to suggest lunacy, you have only to ask me to go and I shall go at once. I got in there by mistake. I don't say it's easy to get in, I don't say such mistakes occur often, but I do say that once you are in it's the very devil to get out, in fact the way I took is about the only way. Are you good at climbing?'

"'Not very,' I said.

"'Well, you see, I am rather,' he said, wagging his head sideways at the plum-tree against the garden-wall. 'The trouble all started over a spell,' he continued. 'Some people believe in spells, some disbelieve them, but I feel you are not one of those who think a man crazy merely because he has believed in a spell.'

"'No, no,' I said.

"'I am glad of that,' said the stranger, 'because I should like to ask your advice when I've told my story, and I naturally wish to avoid saying anything that might give you the kind of idea about me that it is their métier to have at the Home.'

"'No, no,' I said. 'I've met with spells myself.'

"'I'm glad of that,' he repeated. 'This was a spell that I came on quite accidentally, in a Persian manuscript, that was given me by an Arab for a surprisingly simple service, at the foot of the mountains that bound the Sahara. I had merely pointed out to him a snake that he had not seen. I really wasn't thinking of the Arab at all, but only of the beauty of the snake, a brilliant green on the grey roots of a tree, and bars on it like shadows falling on grass, and little else that was green to be seen for miles. I pointed it out, and apparently just in time, for the Arab got the idea that I'd been sent to Africa for that purpose; and so he gave me his greasy bundle of beautiful manuscript, all like swords among flowers. And I could read Persian. But I must have read that spell four times over, before I suddenly saw its amazing import. It was nothing less than a charm to take you back through time. I need hardly say that I was as surprised, when I understood it, as a pigmy of the Congo forest would be at a first class ticket of Cook's, from his home to Victoria station, if he could have understood that. Well, I have not come here to excite your wonder, but to tell you what happened to me when the spell worked. Yes, it worked right enough. I went back.'

"Now I had had some experience of spells, though only African ones, far cruder affairs than the Persian; and I was anxious to get from him the most accurate details. He, on the other hand, after being thought mad for years, yearned now for the commonplace as much as I did for wonder. At any rate he would tell me next to nothing of the magical part of his story, frankly saying that he feared I might think him mad if he did; as though one could brush aside the entire history of spells with the simple remark that a man who believes one is mad.

"Well, back he went. I could get little more out of him than that. He went back about the year 1925, and he went back forty years. Back to antimacassars and overmantels, and a lot of things we have lost; and the high bicycle, that was already threatening the world with change, but with only the faintest hint which nobody saw; and railway trains and many other machines that already held the field, though few guessed yet that they had conquered, and that they were victorious even then over man. I imagine that he made friends, and found his circle, very much as a man might do who arrived in England from some far colony, when he had just grown up. But cross-examination I daren't attempt, not that it made him the least excited to be questioned at all closely, but it clearly alarmed him, his object being to tell me things that I could not doubt, rather than risk any suspicions in the direction in which he was so sensitive.

"'I was just past sixty,' he said. 'And I went back to twenty-one. You know, one's liable to be a little assertive at about that age. Even when one knows nothing, one is a bit proud of one's knowledge when one is twenty-one. But I knew more about several things than the whole civilized world. Wireless, X-rays, motors and flying had never been dreamed of. I know that I should have kept it to myself, I know that I was often not tactful; there were moments, I know, when my exhibition of knowledge amounted to vulgar display; I see all that now. But I was young and I couldn't respect my neighbours' ignorance, though I should have known that it meant as much to them as my scraps of various knowledge did to me. So I talked; I used to deride their poor ten-miles-an-hour on roads, and I talked of all the wonders that were to be. I couldn't put a motor together or make a wireless, then any more than I could now, but whenever I came across anyone who knew anything of machinery I used to talk to them of such things, for I was burning to get them started. Why I was so keen I can't make out. Those were beautiful times, and we've spoiled them; we've spoiled them with too much noise and too much hurry; we've let machinery loose on them. I'd seen it all; I knew the mistake we'd made; yet the moment I got back there I felt bound to teach them, bound to commit them to the very course I often so much deplore. Luckily for them they couldn't understand me, but that only goaded me on to fiercer efforts. I explained wireless and X-rays and flying to them till I thought they must understand, and yet I knew no more of these things than the average man of today knows, if he is not an expert at any of them. And another great difficulty I had was to express the little I knew, to the folk of an age in which none of the technical terms of motoring, wireless or flying had yet been invented.

"'I had my living to earn, but I somehow couldn't even get started at that until I'd told them the things I knew. I couldn't even see a rutted road without criticizing it. It would have been much better to have said nothing. Those were quiet and happy days; a little of them remains in the corners of old gardens, where they look as though they were hiding; but not much.' And he looked wistfully at a blackbird that had slipped in the stillness on to the top of the wall.

"'Well, I preached against that ancient calm that we had,' he continued. 'I must have been awed by the power lying there unknown by man's hand, or perhaps it was vanity that drove me to tell of my knowledge, or irritation at the childish arguments that they always would bring against it, or perhaps it was mere folly. Whatever it was, I preached of the new wonders, till there came a day when I noticed that people were getting odd ideas about me. It's wonderful how an idea spreads: within a day or two of noticing that anyone had a queer idea about me I began to see that they all had. There was no mistaking it, once I had noticed it. I'm not quite sure what started it; but what clinched it was a rather curious thing, and it told against me more than anything else, because doctors and people with any scientific knowledge always went for it, and in the end it was what did for me. This was a thing I had said about wireless: I had told them that it would be possible to get the right time sent out over the whole country. They said that sound without wires, whatever one did, must take about a hundred minutes to go the length of England and Scotland, if it got there at all; that was the pace of sound. And I said it could do it in the two hundredth part of a second. You see, there was a considerable discrepancy, and they got heated about it. Unscientific people hated my talk; scientific ones said sound travelled under two hundred yards in a second. Well, to make a long story short, they certified me; and I played tennis on that court that you must have seen, for about forty years. It was one of the earliest lawn-tennis courts made in England.'

"'For forty years!' I said.

"He nodded his head.

"'But when wireless and flying came in? All the things that you'd prophesied.'

"'One thing governs the world,' he answered.

"'One thing?' I muttered.

"'One thing,' he repeated. 'One thing outside the walls of the Home. Inside it is doubly important. Tact.'

"'Well, yes,' I agreed.

"'I hadn't enough of it,' he said sadly. 'Too much of the spirit of the reformer I suppose. That's a curse for the reformer, whatever it is for the world. I hadn't enough tact.'

"'What happened?' I asked. For he was silently brooding.

"'When wireless and flying came in I said, "I told you so." That was fatal: I soon saw that. You don't get out of those homes by annoying the warders.'

"'But did nobody see you were right?' I asked

"'The chaplain told me it was bad form to say "I told you so." That was all I got out of that.'

"He thought for a while and went on: 'I had only one card left.'

"'What was that?' I said.

"'Climbing,' he answered. 'And it was years before I pulled off that. It was a stiff job. And now,' he added more cheerily, 'I have come to ask your advice, the advice of someone with an outside point of view, someone that has never played tennis on that court of ours at the Home.'

"'I should be delighted to give you,' I said, 'any advice that I can.'

"'I hid the spell,' he said. 'I have got it still. The Persian manuscript, and the spell that takes you back. I buried it, and I know where to find it. Shall I go back again?'

"I shook my head.

"'But I shouldn't speak of the wonders this time,' he said. 'I am getting old, and it's time I went back. I shouldn't say a word of wireless or flying. I've learned my lesson.'

"'Men never learn,' I said. 'You'd do it again. You couldn't help it when you got back there.' He had been calm till now, but now he gesticulated as he appealed to me, and the more excited he got, the more I stuck to my point.

"'I'd try not to say a word to them,' he said after a while.

"And when I heard the word 'try' I knew he was giving way.

"'You couldn't help it,' I said again. 'Think what a quiet age it was. It was broken up by these wonders. Don't go and try to spoil it before its time.'

"I really don't know why I took him so seriously. But somehow I didn't seem to have any choice. I don't know how he did it, but he imposed my valuation of him upon me. But, for all that, he took my advice. I have no doubt of that whatever. He looked round that quiet old garden and up at the darkening trees, and making a kind of gesture with both his hands, that I knew was renunciation, he went back by the way that he came."

Stranger Than Fiction

As Jorkens finished a tale one day at the club, and there was a momentary silence among us while we turned it over in our minds, Terbut, who could find nothing in the tale against which he could bring any proof, said with what I fear may have been an unfriendly suggestion, "Have you ever tried your hand at fiction?"

But Jorkens, who was not the man to make trouble on account of a doubtful suggestion, thought for a moment, and then said, "Only once."

"You wrote a story?" said Terbut.

"Not even that," replied Jorkens. "I only made notes of it. That is as near as I ever got to fiction."

And, whatever Terbut's intention may have been, he had got his answer and there seemed no more for him to say. But he persisted until he got at the facts, and I am rather glad he did, for they showed a curious episode in the varied experience of Jorkens.

"Was the idea a good one?" said Terbut next.

"It was a magnificent idea," said Jorkens. "It was one of those ideas that come to one, or not, as they please. There's no working them out. If such an idea doesn't come, you go without it. I never got another. I am not the kind of man that ideas usually come to. I've travelled and seen things, and I'm all for facts. But at least when this idea did come I recognized the magnificence of it. I dare say it might have made a play or a poem; but I was going to write it plain as a tale. I dare say my technique would not have been very strong. But what of that? They would have recognized the splendour of the idea through any imperfections of workmanship. It would have made a wonderful story. I should have been hailed as a new writer. I should have written more stories and settled down to a writer's comfortable life, inventing whatever I pleased, instead of wandering the world to find a curious thing here and an odd custom there, in heat and sandstorms and flies. Well, well.

"The moment I got the idea I jotted it down. And the next thing I did was to translate my notes into a cypher that nobody knew but me; then I burnt my first notes. I wasn't going to have anyone going off with my idea. You know what writers are: if one of them had got to hear of an idea like that, he'd have grabbed it."

"And did you lose the key of the cypher?" broke in Terbut, with a glint in his eye as though he had spoiled Jorkens' story by anticipating the point of it.

"No," said Jorkens, "and it wouldn't have mattered if I had, for I could never have forgotten that story; it was too striking, too grim, too Greek: it had the very tread of Nemesis in it, the echo of the footstep of Fate pursuing presumptuous man."

"Then you remember it?" said Terbut.

"I shall always remember it," answered Jorkens.

And Terbut quietly played what he thought was a winning card, with the air of a man playing the fourth ace, not knowing that the pack on that particular evening has five of them. "Then you will tell it us," said Terbut.

"Oh yes," said Jorkens. "It was about a man who undergoes the Voronoff treatment, and thinks that he has found his lost youth again, and struts about in front of his friends, and slaps himself on the chest to show them how strong he is. And strutting before his friends isn't enough for him; he hires some great hall, I hadn't quite thought of the Albert Hall, but a big hall any way; and he is going to tell them all how strong he is, and how to live to a hundred. Then the day comes, and there's the shadow of Fate stalking him; only about a dozen people have come to hear him; and he's hired a hall that will hold eight or nine thousand. Think of his audacity and his fervour, and then those lines and lines of desolate seats and the audience of twelve, their interest killed by the emptiness, if they even ever felt any interest at all. Fate makes those contrasts sometimes. But this was only the shadow of Fate: there was more than that in wait for this man's presumption. My idea was that that slap on the chest, to show his strength, was too much for him; and, that when the little audience is seated, the manager comes to the platform, and announces that the man who was to address them is dead."

"Not very probable," was Terbut's comment.

"Probable!" exclaimed Jorkens. "It was much too near probability."

And as none of us quite understood him, no one said anything.

"There was something tremendous in it," went on Jorkens.

"Yes," said Terbut. "But why didn't you write it?"

"Too late," said Jorkens bitterly.

"Too late? Did someone else write it?" Terbut asked.

"Someone else?" exclaimed Jorkens. "Never! An idea like that comes never to two men. Why! It's an inspiration. A man may copy it consciously or unconsciously if it gets out. There've been cases of two men at the same idea, but then the idea was in the air, and in typescript too. Mine was in cypher and locked up, and there was no other copy."

"Then why not write it?" Terbut persisted.

"I was too slow," said Jorkens. "I thought I could wait as long as I liked. You can seldom do that with anything. I knew that no human mind would ever get the same idea; but there was a competitor I had never dreamed of, never considered for a single instant, and it got me as the tortoise got the hare, though a tortoise is a hundred times too tiny a beast to suggest the shattering ending of my only effort at fiction."

"Well, if nobody wrote it," said Terbut, "I can't see what's to prevent you writing it yet."

"It happened," said Jorkens.

"Happened?" said Terbut.

"Word for word as I told you," Jorkens said. "He took the Albert Hall; and reporters jotted down what a poet would never have thought of."

The Golden Gods

"I put them back! I put them back!" shouted Jorkens.

We had finished our lunch long ago; a few were lingering at the table still, and one or two were sitting before the fire, rather listless on a dull November day before the waiter had turned up the lights; but Jorkens was fast asleep.

"Put what back?" asked Terbut, who was seated near him.

And Jorkens turned and stared into his face, with widely opened eyes, and said, "The sack-full of sapphires."

"What sapphires?" stuttered Terbut, astonished at the certainty with which Jorkens made his reply, as though no question of anything else but sapphires should have entered anyone's head.

"Why, it's Terbut," said Jorkens, with so heavy a sigh of relief that the mystification of Terbut was only deepened.

"And who did you think . . . ?" began Terbut. But Jorkens only shook his head, and so silently, that Terbut's question somehow faded away.

All was quiet again, where we rested after our lunch, and I had the impression that Jorkens would have returned to his sleep but that he somehow dared not. So things remained, until Terbut, his old self once more, suddenly said to Jorkens: "Where are those sapphires?"

And Jorkens turned again and looked at him, wide awake this time.

"I'd almost tell you, Terbut," he said. "But you don't really mean any harm."

That puzzled me too, and Terbut, and all the rest. While we were wondering what he meant, Jorkens suddenly began his tale.

"There's a country not so very far away, as remote lands go. Three days from Victoria station and you are looking out on a land growing gradually savage, gradually inhospitable to man, all the bright morning; until in the afternoon it becomes ferocious. That is, if the boat is punctual at Alger and you catch the evening train. The earth becomes savager and savager, till you wouldn't think it would tolerate life either in man or beast, but there are still flocks grazing there; and then in the afternoon you come to a sudden wall, a sheer garden wall made out of mountains, and on one side is the land they are pleased to call the Tel, by which they mean land that an Arab can eke some sort of a living from: on the other side lies the Desert. From the south of that garden wall a rumour had come, and gone quick enough to the coast, and had hung about there in the towns, Lord knows how long, until one day it slipped across to Provence, and I heard it there in the hills: a wandering singer told it me by the road, as I stood and watched the evening come down upon distant Alps. And the rumour told of treasure in one of Sahara's mountains, a mountain out in the desert by itself, like a little rock on a path. Not very far in.

"Well, of course I've heard lots of rumours in my time; and one likes to hear them; they cheer the imagination. But a traveller doesn't act on them. Bradshaw and the map are more what one wants; as far as they go. But there was one very curious thing about this rumour; there were details, lots of them, such as you scarcely ever find in rumours; things like latitude and longitude, and names of places, and distances; and trifles, as they seem to one here, like where to get water. And, mind you, it was an old singer that was telling it to me, a man who got his living in little villages by flights of fancy and poetical melodies, and in a strange old patois: if one got hard facts from such a man as that, and through all that out-of-date patois, there was bound to be plenty of truth in it. You see, his tendency would be all the other way, a man like that wouldn't care for geographical facts, he would tend to get away from them; and the same with the patois, it wasn't made for scientific data; so any I got would be there in spite of the man and his dialect. You quite see what I mean."

And we certainly did at the time. Looking back on it his argument does not seem so entirely conclusive; or it may be that I have not remembered all its points exactly as Jorkens gave them.

"So," Jorkens continued, "I saw that this was a rumour on which one could act. I even had the altitude of the mountain. And the treasure was immense. The only flaw I could see at all in the rumour was that the man had never gone to look for the treasure himself. I asked him why not, and he said: 'I have my songs to sing.'

"Well, there and then I decided to try. Who wouldn't?

"I never knew whether that wandering singer had liked my stopping to talk to him on the road, and taking an interest in his songs, and had wished to reward me; or whether he had hated to see a stranger walking his favourite road and breaking in with a clumsy foreign accent on his eccentric and probably narrow thoughts: one does not know another man's point of view half as often as one supposes.

"It may have been that; it may well have been."

And Jorkens gazed into the fire awhile, wondering.

"Well, I went," said Jorkens. "I didn't even return to London, but started off from Marseilles; and the evening of the day after that I was dining in a train going southwards from Alger. There'd been a landslip in some mountains, I remember; and the train was held up awhile; then it went on again. And we passed a gang of men that had let us through: they just looked up at the train as it went by; I wonder if anyone but I looked down at them. I remember the lanterns shining, and the look in the men's faces; then the night again.

"In the morning bright sunlight woke me through the narrowest crack of the blind, and when I pulled it up there was the beautiful earth, with a frown gathering on its features and deepening as we went southwards, a sternness that was not yet sheer savage desert, but a hint of what was before us. And in the afternoon the battlements and the spires of the mountains that border the desert rose strange and bright as a tale by Scheherazade.

"Just there, with a sudden luxuriance, before a thousand miles of aridity, earth lavished a forest of palm-trees; and in the village that this surprising wealth supported there dwelt an Arab I knew. I had written to him and he was to meet me at this station and join the train, having sent on my little camp with five or six other Arabs and three camels about fifty miles into the desert; and the train would bring us to within fifteen miles of them, an easy walk in those days; oh dear me! I knew that I could rely on Ismail; so that the third night after leaving Marseilles I should sleep in the desert, for whose vast calm I was yearning after the weariness and fret of the trains. And there sure enough he was, and somehow I knew from his attitude as he sat, that he had been sitting on that platform for several hours, waiting without impatience. He had believed me when I wrote that I would arrive by train on that day, but to predict the precise hour of the train's arrival, or of any event whatever, was not the affair of man. We greeted: it was long since we had met. And then I asked him of the little caravan: it was gone to the appointed place; the serenity of his answer contrasted with the fuss and noise of my journey. Then I tried to hurry him to his place in the train and he strode slowly away.

"I had not told Ismail I was seeking for hidden treasure, and but for one thing I should never have credited myself with the ability to keep such a secret as that from the Arabs. That one thing was a perfectly genuine devotion to the sport of big-game-hunting. No excuse would have eluded half a dozen Arabs for a month in the desert; but

Ismail and I knew each other already as hunters, and few trophies that a hunter can get are more to be prized than the great head of an arui, with its massive horns and huge beard, provided one picks one's head as a hunter should, in fact he is not a hunter otherwise. The ovis poli and the ovis ammon are larger, but the arui (as the Arabs call him) is the one African sheep; and, if the value of a trophy depend on size, beauty and hard work, I know no trophy in all the plains of Africa that can equal this prize of the mountains."

"I'd put risk as one of the ingredients in valuing a trophy," said someone.

"Yes," said Jorkens. "Well, the lion has his teeth, the rhino his horn, the buffalo his brains and the old arui his precipices; any way it's a good trophy, and the place I was going to was one of the likeliest spots for it in Africa; I'd been within fifty miles of it with Ismail before, and fifty miles in that sort of country is like walking across the street here. That's why I'd started at once; I knew the country and knew the man to get me there, and had a perfectly good reason for going, which he would never see through; it was so genuine a reason that it was practically opaque.

"Well, we started out of the station with Ismail safe in the train, and passed through the mighty gateway, the pillars of which are two mountains; and far below me I saw the desert again, bright blue, as ever."

"Blue?" Terbut muttered, but Jorkens was gazing into the fire, his eyes too full of some memory to pay any attention to Terbut.

"We passed two or three stations and came to Les Puits Romains, where Ismail and I were to get out. And I did get out, but the station-master came up before I was down the steps, and said, 'But you are getting out.' 'Yes,' I said. 'But it is Les Puits Romains,' said he. 'Yes, I get out here,' said I. 'You get out?' he asked. And he didn't know what to do. And then he did the only thing that he had the authority to do, and asked to see my ticket, which I showed him. And then he could do no more. So I got out, and Ismail and I walked straight away into the desert and all the heads came out of the windows and watched us walking away, till the train went round a curve and train and heads disappeared. Evidently people did not get out at Les Puits Romains.

"And the surprise that all these folk showed me was dancing in my veins too, when I felt the desert under my feet after all these hours of train, as I came suddenly upon something calm and everlasting from fretful ephemeral machinery. I took out my watch to see what time it was, and suddenly realized that time no longer mattered to me, and put my watch back in my pocket. We had my rifle with us, and Ismail had promised the chance of edni, a rare gazelle, in the hills. We found no edni that day, but how much it was even to be looking for one, coming, as I was, straight out of a restaurant car; and how much it is to look back from here, today, and to think that once I got my own food with my rifle and ate it in the Sahara, while here you can't get even a drink without buying it, and there are houses and pavement all round one for hundreds and hundreds of miles."

There are certain moods in Jorkens that lead almost to tears, though you wouldn't think it to hear him talking away, and those moods are not only saddening to Jorkens, but they have an uncanny knack of affecting others, and I have known myself to be quite depressed by them; I say this to disclaim the intention of exhibiting any generosity, when I record that I offered Jorkens a whiskey which he did not have to buy. Very often if you can upset one point in any complaint that a man may be making against the world, you may show him that the whole thing is not so bad as he thought. It was certainly so in this case. Jorkens thanked me with no more than a nod, and drank in silence; but when he had drunk, and put the glass carefully down, he said: "Not a bad place, London." And for some while he did not want to return to his story. When he did return to it he returned with a cheerfulness of which I was glad to be, however slightly, the cause.

"When I saw my own tent and the Arabs' little encampment, and the Sahara lying all round it, I said: 'Back again!' It felt like coming home, back after ages and ages to some home that time had never affected at all. Do you know what I mean? Some house you knew years ago, bright walls, and the windows shining, and the level rays of a long summer's evening; then time freezes and it stays like that for ever, and years after you meet it again. Can you imagine that?"

"Wait a moment," said Terbut. "I'll have a drink too."

But Jorkens was too far back again in the past and in the Sahara to see any implied criticism.

"Well," said Jorkens, "it was just like that. Here I was back again. And the sun set and the desert flashed into pink, and a horde of mountains away to the east were blue, and the desert lashed rose at them and the colour of peonies. Soon all that host of mountains were pink and purple, but for a few that stood like pillars of pure gold; every moment brought some change no painter could have kept pace with; and either a cold wind blew or an awe from the mountains chilled me, for that distant company seemed about to murmur some secret that would have been audible over the desert from their tremendous voices; but just then they cloaked themselves with azure cloaks and seemed to move further away, as though they planned some deed that was only the business of mountains. A little while and all the colour was gone, and nothing remained of the splendour of that gathering of the mountains, whose secret had seemed for a moment to be so close to utterance, nothing but a blush in the sky under which their shapes had vanished. And then the Arabs prayed; and after each had prayed, they did what I have seldom known them do, they sat in a little semi-circle facing Mecca, except Ismail who sat facing them; and they all intoned some psalm in which Ismail led them. They have fine voices, and it's very odd how like the sound of one religious service is to the sound of any other, in any part of the world: of course you won't mention that outside the club; they hate each other so much that they'd none of them like it; but there it is, and the sound of them chanting, outside my tent in the dusk, called up the scene of a cathedral at evening, and the thought of a cathedral called up a city, and the loneliness seemed to have suddenly gone from the desert. For a quarter of an hour I listened, and all the while I had the feeling of something populous, something metropolitan, possessing the air all round me, while they chanted after Ismail towards Mecca. But far more imposing than this, more memorable than the music of their voices, perhaps more tremendously impressive than any other experience that ever overtook me, was the return of the silence of the desert when they had done. It came back like a wave breaking, like a whole ocean covering suddenly a land full of cities and people."

"Yes, silence is impressive," said Terbut.

"You've never known it," said Jorkens, and continued his story. "And then the stars came out huge and white, and the Arabs lit a fire to cook their kous-kous, as they call a dish that they make of flour and rancid oil and sand. And I went and sat by the fire and they told me the names of their stars. The Great Bear for instance; his name is Nash, and he is being carried to the grave-yard on a stretcher; you can see the four stretcher-bearers. And his wife and his mother and sister are walking behind, and they pointed to what you better-educated people know to be the handle of the plough. But what impressed me most about the story of Nash was when they turned round to the other horizon and pointed to a star that was just peering over the edge, and said: 'That's the one that did it!' And sure enough it had just popped up and within an hour was gone again, a slinking and murderous-looking star.

"Soon I made a few plans with Ismail and went to bed. My plans were these: we were camped about the end of a range of mountains running roughly westwards, and I would hunt along this range. When I had done twenty miles of it I should come opposite another range, out by itself in the desert, only a few miles away, running parallel. It was barely ten miles long, but pretty steep, and at the top of one of its precipices was the treasure. It seemed to me, from what I could find out of the shape of it, a very good ground for arui. And here I would never go of my own free will. I would hunt the longer range that was not so high or steep, until the game were beginning to leave it, and I would only go to the better ground when persuaded to do so by Ismail. I think I told you that I had not explained to any of them that I was out looking for treasure: it's no use having one's throat quietly cut in the night. I liked Ismail, but treasure is treasure. And if I had to have my throat cut by anyone I'd have it done by Ismail, for his way with a sheep was amazing; but I saw no need to tell him about the treasure.

"I forget how long the Sahara lulled me before I fell asleep; but I remember that wonderfully soon, as it seemed, I was awakened by someone praying, and while my tent was still dark, though when one of them brought me some tea a few minutes later I saw through my opened tent-door a glow on the mountains, and all the stars were gone. How it lingers with me still, our little camp in the morning, the dew all pearly on the hair of the camels, and Ismail waiting to start for the rosy mountains. These were days when I almost forgot the treasure. It seemed enough to be up in the clear bright morning, breathing that brilliant air, to go by winding ravines to inner vales of the mountains, to climb by galleries of statuary, carved out of stone by the storm, to peaks from which the desert, blue as the sea, looked like a huge curved piece of an unfamiliar planet; at evening to come down the slopes and find my tent below me. And on days on which I got one of the arui, and as the pile of great heads began to increase in my camp, what need had I of any other treasure? But the day came when Ismail began to recommend the other range, now very near my camp, standing huge and lonely out by itself in the desert. I would not go, but stuck to the range I was hunting. And a week more went by, and the five last days of it were blank, days in which we never even saw an arui, and I said, 'Where are there any?' in the tone of voice that implied there were no more Barbary sheep left in Africa; and Ismail, who knew their ways and lived for hunting them, answered indignantly that they were in the range to which I would not go, flinging out an arm towards it. And nothing was left for me then but to go to the mountain in which the treasure lay. Next day we started, walking across the desert, and coming, Ismail and I, in an hour or so to the mountain. There was no mistaking that height that had been described to me as rising up like a tower out of the desert: there were inner peaks that were higher, but, looking at it where we stood, it seemed to go right up from desert to sky, though a moment's reflection showed that it could not be the highest point of the range, because a long smooth curve on its summit was clearly the mouth of a river that had once gone over the top of it. And below this curve of the riverbed, in the face of the cliff, were the little black marks of the caves that I had been told to look for, three caves set apart from each other by little rocky pillars, which must have been veiled from sight altogether when the torrent came over the cliff. I saw at a glance that it was a difficult, though not impossible, climb. But what could I tell by a glance? I could not tell that it was a mountain that should only be climbed by night; it seemed too obviously a climb that could be managed only by day. And so I planned to climb it there and then, my chief consideration, on which I had spent much thought overnight, being how to climb it alone. You can't say to your hunter in a desert, 'Well, we part here. I've some things to see to, or a friend to call on, up that mountain.' But I told Ismail I was tired of looking for arui, and finding none for five days, and that I had little faith in this new range of his, so I would go up that mountain and wait over the top of it somewhere about the middle of the range, while he should go to the eastern end, only about three miles away, and climb it and come along the tops of the hills to me, driving any arui that he met before him. It took some time to persuade him to so bad a plan, for, to begin with, the top of the range was a mile wide, so that, even if I could shoot four hundred yards each way, I still left half of it unguarded; and the arui need not come along the tops at all. But in the end I persuaded him, and he flapped an end of his burnous over his shoulder and went away rather sulkily. I had to keep my rifle, which was a nuisance, but it had a sling to it, and I slung it across my back.

Well, it was ordinary mountaineering for the first thousand feet, but as I began to approach the caves I found myself following a certain well-defined track, in fact either to left or right an ascent seemed impossible, and on each side of this track, which was only six feet across, there were holes every yard in the rock, which had clearly been bored by man. And all these holes evidently sheltered snakes. Whether the makers of the holes had known so well the habits of snakes, and had shaped the holes accordingly and known that the snakes would come; or whether they had abundantly stocked the holes with snakes and left them there to breed, I shall of course never know, but the slope that I climbed was grey with them; little grey snakes no longer than a rabbit, as swift as a greyhound and deadly as a tiger. I didn't like it at all.

"But it wasn't the snakes. I don't know what I may have shouted in my sleep. I hope I didn't make too much noise. But it wasn't the snakes. There was a trifling incident of the climb that I should have told you; I don't remember where it occurred; but I remember that somewhere I got hold of a rock to pull myself up by, a thing about the size of a wheelbarrow, and the rock began to give; it was coming away. Well I had to push it back and get it steady again; I was just below it, you see. It took some time and caution, and then I went on. That was all. That was all, at the time. And then I came to the caves, which were very low; I could just crawl in; and when I was inside, where the roof was a bit higher, I saw they were really one, though the two pillars made them seem three from outside. And an idol of solid gold was sitting over a basin, and two other golden gods on his left and right were seated each before a basin too. And on the ground below each basin was a scroll covered in writing in quite a dozen languages. One of the languages was latin and another arabic; and it evidently said the same in all the languages. It was a list of curses, a different lot for each bowl; there wasn't any doubt, unless you absolutely disbelieved in all curses, and in all the powers of all heterodoxical gods, that these curses were the price of the bowls. You could take any bowl you liked, when you'd climbed the cliff and come by the grey snakes, but you got the curses. And the three bowls, or basins, were all full of precious stones. There were rubies in one and emeralds in another, but I didn't fancy the curses. And in the middle one of the three were sapphires, with the squat god gazing down at them. I took that one. The curse of that one was the memory of the climb, a memory haunting dreams. All the curses dealt with dreams. I took it and emptied it into a haversack that I carried, and left the copper basin empty before the god.

"The fifty feet above me was sheer, worn smooth by a bygone torrent, so I went back past the grey snakes and found my way to the top by another slope, and took up a position, bent only on satisfying Ismail that an arui was my sole motive. And sure enough one came. He came past about three hundred yards away, and I began by missing him; and then I saw one bullet sending the dust up under him, and I aimed over his back, and of course yards in front, and with the next but one I dropped him. And I went up to it and waited for Ismail, rejoicing that any suspicion in his mind would now be impossible. But I forgot the golden gods.

"I forgot the golden gods, but I was soon to remember them. We covered the arui with rocks and came down the mountain, Ismail in cheerful mood; and we crossed the strip of desert and were back in my camp before evening. Then came tea, which is one of the events of the day, tea with jam that I had brought out with me; and after that I sat in a canvas chair and watched the changing glory of the sunset revelling in the east on the rosy faces of mountains. I remember it was a strange sunset; not only did mountains I knew seem totally different, but hills I had never seen came suddenly close, and distant rocks shone brightly vividly clear, as though they had only just been placed on the scene as a setting for this drama of the sunset that has no point to us, but that may, for all we know, be full of immense significancies. I remember the splendour with which a storm was getting up in the desert; the Sahara its darkest blue, purple clouds sweeping past the peony-coloured mountains that stood in a Cambridge-blue sky, and riding down to the butt end of a rainbow that stood like a tower far off, and turning to rose as they neared it."

"Like that, was it?" said one of us, staring out into the fog and hardly believing so much light could be lawful.

"For twenty seconds it was," said Jorkens. "And every twenty seconds or so it changed completely, clouds and colour and mountains. Yet all the while it seemed to hold something ominous, the very air was thrilled with it. And when all the colour was gone, but for a ruddy band along the western horizon, the desert seemed to be leering at me for twenty miles with a wink of one red eye. Then I emptied my sapphires into an old sack that I had, in which I had been collecting flint implements; for the desert is full of the worked flints of an earlier people, flints I had learned to pick up on the North downs once as a boy;

and, whatever difference there was between ancient Briton and ancient dweller in what is now the Sahara, the flint took the same shape in the same way, in Africa as in Kent, under those ancient blows. The Arabs not only noticed my peculiarity of picking up stones of this particular shape, but were very soon picking them up for me themselves. So that everything was ready for the concealment of my sapphires, and in a country where so little is overlooked that I cannot ever remember, in fifty camps, a safety-pin or a bootlace being left behind when striking one's tent in the Sahara. I threw a few flints on top, and tied up the neck of the sack; and very soon after that I went to bed. The storm that had been striding up through the sunset broke about then, with a wind that must have been roaring down the ravine in which we were camped, but I could hear no sound of anything but the crash of the rain on my tent. It kept me awake awhile, but not long enough. Not nearly long enough. I was tired with my day on the mountain and slept as one does, living that life, and in that air. I slept, and the curse of the golden gods, that was written on parchment, came down on me.

"I told you that a big rock, by which I was about to lift myself, loosened. I had not thought again of it all day: such things frequently happen. But now by night I saw the rock more vividly than I can ever have had time to notice it. I felt the feel of its rough surface, that gives such a good foothold, as my hands got hold of its edges. I felt myself trusting my weight to it. And then I felt the tremor in the rock, now right in front of my face, that taught me it was not firm and was coming away, taught me that, far from holding me safe from the great emptiness lying below me, it was I that must hold this rock in its ancient place, watching its long watch on a cliff of that forsaken mountain. If it fell it would partially crush me, and roll what was left down a slope of a thousand feet. I had not the whole weight of the rock to hold in its place: that would have been impossible. But I had pulled it half an inch past its point of balance, and had felt in time what I had done. But was it in time? I could not get out of its way. Had I been standing on good firm ground I could have easily pushed it back, but one does not cling with both one's hands to a rock if one has good ground beneath one. I pushed the rock gently; I had not the foothold to do any more than that; and I nearly got it back again. But fragments of dry earth and grains of sand had poured into the crack between the rock and the cliff, and it would not quite go back. I got it on to its very point of balance, but as soon as I drew my hand away it rocked, and my own foothold was barely secure. I felt the awful emptiness below me, till the soles of my feet thrilled with it. Never, never, never can I forget the tremor that I felt in the rock, or the terrible clarity with which I understood the depth of the drop beneath me. These things are burned by that dream into my brain for ever. For hours I clung there, for the greater part of the day, till I knew all the minutest markings on the whole of the rock's surface; and towards evening I began to think that the other rocks were watching me, and I thrust the thought away, determining to die sane. It had begun at dawn and I was still there late in the evening, and suddenly the tremor in the rock had ceased; it had sunk back to its old bed or had accepted the new one in which I had held it so long. I climbed carefully past it, and then, with a brief exultation that the idols allowed to my dream, I sped up to the cave in which the treasure lay. All the bowls were full, and all sparkling at me, and no parchments with curses on them lay anywhere near, but the moment I entered the curse worked again, coming down on me at the feet of the golden gods. I told you the cave was low; but when I entered it in my dream the oppression was overwhelming. There was perhaps not more than fifty feet of sheer mountain above me, but fifty feet of solid mountain is a terrifying thing to contemplate, and I was conscious of every ton of it. It was not like being in a trap or a snare, a light thing and of human devising, but above that low roof was a force wrenched once from ancient Chaos, a thing of which planets are made. But no words I can use could ever make you feel the faintest chill of that fear from which I suffered, or make you see even the shadow of it, a fear of being gripped by Earth itself, and held and suffocated there in darkness. I can only say that never since that night have I been able to enter any narrow space, or even a very small room, without being overcome by acute terror. It isn't a thing I can explain; I don't even know who wrote the parchment out; but for the whole of that stormy night the curse gripped me, and rocked me between two terrors, the awful terror of the falling stone, and the terror of the grim and frightful weight of the mountain. I was never free of them, they came back again and again, and with all that waste of hours at their disposal that dreams seem to have, being able to condense time in some horrible way, so that you can never escape from them by mere waiting, by the mere ticking of the clock. It may have been months, in dreamland, before dawn came; and I know I was aged far more than by the length of a single night.

"The sound of Ismail praying outside my tent in the dawn was amongst the blessedest sounds of the few that are stored away to brighten my poor old memory. It brought me back at last from that long period of suffering, whose intensities I can never describe to you, and guided me safely across the terrible borders of dreamland. How I greeted him when he brought me my tea! And he thought my delight came from the arui I had shot yesterday, which seemed ages and ages away and minutely trivial.

"Well, nothing remained but to invent a story for Ismail to account for a journey alone again to the caves, for I was not going to spend another night like that. I packed the sapphires back again in the haversack and into my pockets, pretending that they were lunch, and actually taking no food at all. And the story I told Ismail was a poor one, but it did not need to be so good as it had to be when there was actually treasure in my tent to conceal; whatever he suspected this time, he could never find any treasure, as I was taking it back to the gods. One such night was enough. I told Ismail I had found flint implements up in the mountain, and that I would not shoot today, and I was going to look for more flints. I don't know if he believed me, or what he thought I was going to do: I don't know Arabs well enough to know how they look when they doubt you. Four Arabs were going back to the mountain to bring my arui in, and I hurried them off as soon as possible so as to get them out of the way; but another thing delayed me, and that was the necessity to start the last part of the climb when the sun was low, and the snakes would no longer be lying out on the rocks; for, though I had not worried about the snakes through the long terrors of that dreadful dream, the odds in favour of getting through them were not so long that one wished to try more than once. They were the real danger, in spite of the terror with which the rock and the cave were clothed by the curse of the gods. Well, I crossed the strip of desert and started the climb again. I came to that rock and went carefully round it, but none of those agonies of horror haunted the actual rock that clothed its phantasm with such frightful powers in dreamland and in the dark. I came again to the cave and crawled in, and saw the empty bowl, and emptied back every sapphire and came away.

"It was dark before I came again to the desert, but I had light enough for the worst of the climb. And the first thing I did after I got back to camp was to have a bath in a little shelter of canvas outside my tent, which gave Ismail the opportunity of making any search he pleased, if my rather lame reason for going back to the mountain had awakened any suspicions. That night I slept. The quiet sleep that I so much needed.

"There is little more to tell. We struck camp next day and began our journey back to the railway, and I never saw the golden gods again. Who put them there, who sanctified them, who wrote the curses on parchment, I shall never know now; but I fancy it must have been a long time ago, as several of the languages on the three parchments seemed obsolete. I don't think they'll be there much longer, as the mouth of the river above them had the appearance of working backward, probably an inch or two every year when the winter storms descended, and the face of the cliff would go back with the bed of the river. It's many years ago now: the whole thing has probably gone.

"And a good thing too.

"I never had that dream any more. Not really the dream with the whole force of the parchment. A nightmare now and then such as anybody might have, and sometimes in the nightmare the rock begins to totter. That of course is terrible, but I shout at once, 'I put them back.' Always the same words, and the gods remember. Sometimes they forget for a moment, the fat little devils. But they remember the moment I shout, and I know my reason is safe. But if I hadn't put them back; if I hadn't put them back! Oh, the thing doesn't bear thinking of.

"Waiter!"

The Correct Kit

Ours is a small club; but one day, with some idea of the committee that we should make ourselves a little more important, we unfortunately arranged a big dinner. White ties, speeches and all the rest of it. At least, that was the idea of the committee. White ties we actually had, but the speeches never came off, for in the end we sat listening instead to one of those tales of Jorkens. He, looking round at us all in our starched shirts, had suddenly said: "It reminds me of a cannibal feast I once attended in Africa."

Everyone laughed at that, including me, though I saw no particular point in it. And then Terbut said: "Not quite so many white ties I should imagine."

And we all laughed with Terbut.

When the laughter was over, and Terbut was still smiling quietly to himself, Jorkens began his story.

"Up the Nile, till it loses its name and becomes the White Nile, and into Lake No, and out of that into the Bahr el Gazal, I went once about as far as the Bahr el Arab. I had left the Sahara Desert far behind me, I had left that little piece of English civilization that has been transplanted in Khartoum, and a few hundred miles of the White Nile, and a lake like a melted opal, and the papyrus swamps, and had come to firm ground at last, and the scarlet trunks of trees, and mimosa with its small round yellow flowers shining in the sun, as the sun itself might shine on the planet Neptune. When I saw all this good firm land, I decided to leave my dahabeah and go south for a couple of days, in order to stretch my legs, as much as anything; and in the hope of getting a couple of pairs of tusks, which would about pay for my trip, if they were big enough. And all the elephant tracks I had seen seemed to be leading south. So I took two men and a couple of donkeys and a light camping outfit, and I travelled south for two days without seeing an elephant. On the morning of the third day I was walking along with one Arab, who was carrying my double .470, about a mile from my camp. I was still in the Dinka country, a people I knew quite well, who always struck me as harmless, naked except for grey ash they rubbed into their skins, a blue necklace, and a feather in their hair: the grey ash is to keep off mosquitoes. I was walking along with this Arab, when suddenly I saw to the right and left a number of men with spears who were hurrying away in front of me. Strange though they were to me (and what is strange out there is usually dangerous) they seemed in such a hurry at first to get out of my way, that I let valuable seconds go by before I reached for my rifle, not that I could have done anything against over eighty of them; and, before I could say knife, the two lots met about a hundred yards in front of me, and looking back I saw that I was completely surrounded. Eighty-five men with spears, of a tribe that I did not know, and every one of them in evening dress."

"You mean," said one of us, "they were a bit décolleté."

"No," said Jorkens. "Evening dress."

Then, "What kind of evening dress does a savage wear?" said Terbut.

"White ties, white waistcoats," said Jorkens quietly. "In fact just what you are wearing now, except that they had rather heavier watch-chains, and they all wore diamond solitaires.

"It was no good shooting; they were all round me. I gave up my rifle to the first man that came for it: it looked odd in his hands against his evening dress. Of course I did a good deal of thinking; and the first thing I thought was that I need hardly expect the worst, because, however nasty the spears looked, anything like cannibalism was impossible in decent evening dress, such as they were all wearing. I was wrong there.

"I saw they weren't Dinkas, but they'd come into Dinka country, and I wondered if they knew the Dinka language. I tried it, they did.

"They were taking me to their camp, where we soon arrived; as I knew we should, for their evening dress was so neat and tidy that it could not have been long put on. And it had not been often put on; one could see that too. Then why had it been put on now? Obviously for some ceremonial occasion. But what?

"There was no longer any doubt of the occasion when we came to the middle of their camp. There hung a cauldron that would have held two pigs. A fire was already burning underneath it; and others, also in evening dress, were adding buckets of water to the cauldron as the water that was already in it boiled. I saw then what was prepared for me; it was nothing less than boiling. I don't know that boiling is really any worse than roasting; but somehow we seem to be more familiar with roasting; we are taught about roasting when we are young, when first we are told of Hell, and, knocking about the world as I have done and getting warned now and then, by people who seem to know, that one is getting nearer to it, one is more inclined to face roasting. But boiling seems to me still an idea one could never get used to.

"And now I noticed they were all straightening their ties, and I saw that I must do something pretty quick, or I should be boiled whether I fancied it or not. Well, I talked to their chief man then, in Dinka talk that they knew through trading with Dinkas. What was the cauldron for? For I pretended not to know. But that was no good. I asked him if he didn't know that eating men was wrong, and that the white man punished people that ate men.

"'Ah, the white man. Great man,' he said.

"'He teaches you not to eat men,' I answered.

"'White man can do no wrong,' he said.

"'Well, sometimes perhaps. Just now and then, but not often,' I said. For I thought I was getting along swimmingly.

"'Not when he is in evening dress,' said the savage.

"Do you know, in about five minutes then I got his horrible point of view. The white man, he explained, was often angry, often hasty, often wrong, but in this ceremonial kit, his evening dress, he could not err! I suppose we have a few tenets of that kind; but, suddenly hearing it like that, it seemed to me perfectly frightful. They had got this kit from a trader who had sold the suits to them for gold and ivory. They knew it was the white man's most important dress, and they had the perfectly horrible idea that it sanctified anything. That was why they had put it on.

"Now what chance had I? The boiling water was deep in the cauldron, and they were dancing around it already with their heavy gold watch-chains flapping. It was no good saying any more against cannibalism; it was clearly one of those things that are wrong without a ceremony, but that a ceremony makes all right. Never at any moment of my life did I feel less like laughter than then. But I burst out laughing. I don't like interfering with any man's faith, especially his faith in a white man. But I burst out laughing and pointed at the white ties that these men had bought from the trader.

"'You laugh?' said their chief man simply.

"'Yes,' I said, 'at those ties.' And I pretended to try to stop my laughter, and laughed again.

"'Not correct evening dress?' he asked quickly, like a bride being married in a church that isn't properly licensed.

"'No, no, no,' I said.

"'What wrong?' he asked.

"'Why, those ties,' I said; 'they should go on the shoes, and the bows that you wear on your shoes should go on your collars.' And I began laughing again.

"He hesitated, and I suddenly remembered a tiresome photograph of a group at a dinner that I had attended in London; the photographer had come round afterwards and got signatures from us, ordering a copy, just at that time of the evening when one isn't so sure what one's signing; and the damned photograph had reached me at Khartoum, of all places, and I had stuffed it into a packet in my tent. I suddenly remembered it now; and we had all been wearing black ties. Of course our feet weren't showing."

"But . . ." began Terbut.

"Don't you see," said Jorkens, "that it proved my point, that the black bows on the shoes should be worn on the collar? Of course some more of the swine had raided my camp; and they had brought the whole outfit in. I soon had hold of that photograph, and it did far more than my limited knowledge of Dinka talk could do. And then I was taking off their ties and cutting them all in half, and tying the halves round their feet with a bit of a bow, just where their toes joined on, and I was only just able to make one; and the bows of their shoes I fastened on to their collar studs, doing it all quickly and boldly, as though I did it every day of my life, and handing each man the spare bow, to wear on Sundays. And then I walked away, and my two Arabs came with me."

"You walked away?" said Terbut.

"Yes," said Jorkens, "and that was the last I saw of them."

"Why didn't they catch you again?" he asked.

"Couldn't walk fast enough," said Jorkens.

"Why didn't they run?" persisted Terbut.

But he got no change out of Jorkens. "You try to run," he said, "with the ends of your shoes tied round with evening ties. The ties will come off. And they daren't do anything without their evening dress. Lots of people are like that. If it comes to that, you were once invited to dine at the Mansion House."

"I was," said Terbut full of dignity.

"And I doubt if you'd have dared to go in any kit but the right one."

"Well . . ." said Terbut.

"Exactly," said Jorkens. "Turtle or man, it's all the same."

And the talk degenerated into a discussion as to what was the proper wear for a variety of occasions.

How Ryan Got Out of Russia

"Once again," said Jorkens suddenly, either in answer to some remark that I had not heard or to some fierce memory that awoke in his mind, "once again I must protest that anyone who finds anything unusual in any story that I may ever have happened to tell knows little of the stories that men do tell, daily, hourly, in fact all the time. All the twenty-four hours of every day there is someone telling some tale here in London, not to mention everywhere else, that is far less credible than anything I ever told. Then why do they single me out for what I can only call incredulity? Can you answer me that? No. And can you tell me any tale I have ever told you, that has been definitely disproved in a properly scientific manner? No," he added before giving anyone very much time, not that anyone seemed ready with any case in point. "And I'll tell you what," Jorkens went on; "I'm ready to prove what I say. I'm ready to take anyone now and show him someone within a mile from here who is telling stranger tales than I've ever told, at this very minute. And if he isn't, he'll begin as soon as we ask him. As many of you as you like. Now, who'll come?"

"Very well, very well," Jorkens went on. "You'll none of you come. Then please never say, or allow anyone else to say, that I tell any more unusual tales than other people. Because I've given you an opportunity of putting it to the proof; and you won't take it. Very well. Waiter."

In another moment Jorkens would have settled down to a large whiskey; he would have soothed himself with it; he would then have slept a little: when he awoke he would have forgotten his anger, for he is never angry for long, and with his anger he would have forgotten the whole episode, including the man to whom he offered to take us. I don't say that Jorkens' tales are unusual, or that they are usual; I leave the reader to judge that; but I do say that anyone whose tales were more unusual would certainly have something to tell that was distinctly out of the way. So before Jorkens had caught the waiter's eye, before any whiskey had had time to be brought to him, I said: "That is unsporting of them, Jorkens. You have offered to prove that your stories are not unusual, as stories go. They should give you a chance to prove it. I'll come."

Jorkens looked for a moment a little regretfully in the direction of the screen at the far end of the room, behind which were the waiters, and then said: "Very well." So away we went from the Billiards Club, and soon we were in a taxi, going towards Soho, with Tutton, another member, who at the last moment came too.

I thought that even in the taxi Jorkens was regretting his whiskey, for he sat silent; but when we got to the dingy café to which he had directed the driver, a dark little place called The Universe, and we went in and he saw at once the man he was looking for, he brightened up a good deal. The man was seated alone at one of the tables eating some odd foreign dish. "Look at his forehead," said Jorkens.

"Yes," I said. "He hasn't got one."

"Well, a pair of bulging eyebrows," said Jorkens. "But no forehead. As you say. Not a man to imagine anything."

"Not in the least," I said.

"No, no," said Tutton.

"Very well," said Jorkens.

He took hold of a couple of chairs then, and dragged them up to the man's table, while I brought one for myself.

"A couple of friends," said Jorkens, "who would like to hear your tale." And all at the same moment he made a sign with one finger to a waiter whose home I would have placed as the East of Europe, though I could get no nearer than that; and the sign meant evidently absinthe, for one came. The man had not spoken yet; then he tasted the absinthe; tasted it again, to be sure it was all right; then started at once. "I was in a Russian prison," he said. "The walls were ten feet thick. And I was sentenced to death."

"Begin at the beginning," said Jorkens.

"Sentenced to die next morning, as a matter of fact," the man went on; "so there wasn't much time. And I was working on the mortar round one of the big stones with the edge of a button off my trousers."

"At the beginning," said Jorkens.

"Oh," said the man; and he looked up from his absinthe, his clipped black moustache wet with it, his eyes groping with memory. Then he started again.

"I never knew who I was spying for," he said.

"Tell them how you came to be spying," said Jorkens.

"I got into a chess-club in Paris," said the man. And he took another drink from his glass of absinthe, and it all seemed to come back to him. "It was a dark low sty of a place. I only went there twice. It was only the second time I ever went there that I looked up from the game I was playing, at one of the other tables. I was having a good enough game and getting a bit the best of it, and I turned to look at one of the other tables while my man was making his move, a table level with mine on the other side of the gangway, and got the shock of my life. I saw all of a sudden that one of the two players didn't know the move of the knight. He was moving it anyhow, and his opponent was taking no notice. Well, it wasn't a chess-club.

"I'd been introduced to the place by a man of whom I knew nothing. No help there. The man I was playing with was a chess-player all right, but one summer doesn't make a swallow. I glanced at a few other boards, and saw pretty much the same thing going on as I had seen at the table beside me. Chess was a blind. What did go on there? I was a long way from the door, and I felt most damnably alone."

"You've never told me, you know," said Jorkens, "what you were doing in Paris."

"Just looking round to see what would turn up," said the man.

"Oh well, go on," replied Jorkens.

He took another sip at the absinthe, and went on.

"I began looking round at the door then, and seeing how many men there were sitting between me and it. I couldn't have done anything worse. I couldn't have made myself more conspicuous if I'd made a dash for it. They followed the turn of my eyes, and all seemed to read my thoughts. And a man got up from another table presently, and loafed my way as though he were not coming up to me. But I knew he was. He passed my table, but turned round at once, and spoke to me. "Are you one of us?" he said.

"It was no use saying Yes. You can't invent passwords. They'd have plenty of them all right. I knew the kind of people they were the moment I discovered what they were not.

"So I said, 'No, but I wish to be.'

"It was the only thing to do. But it let me in for a lot of oaths, of which I can tell you nothing; with penalties attached, you know. And I became a member, of the lowest degree, of an association of which I still know practically nothing at all. All I really knew of its aims was that they seemed to be to give orders to members of the degree to which I belonged. And you had to obey those orders. Otherwise, several unpleasant things, behind the screen at the end of that dingy room, the far end from the door of course, and the Seine afterwards.

"Well, I got away from that room, and I went back to Mimi. I haven't told you about Mimi. And I said to her: 'Mimi, that chess-club isn't a chess-club; it's something else, and I've got to leave Paris.'

"And she said at once: 'Don't you go. People like that would be sure to watch you. Don't let them see you trying to get away. It's not safe.'

"And, do you know, she was right. But all I said to her was: 'People like that, Mimi? But I've not told you what they are like.'

"And all she would say was: 'I know that type,' and went on urging me not to try to go.

"She was right, sure enough. They were watching me. I saw Mimi gazing out of the window next morning, and saying nothing; just gazing, till I went up and gazed too. And there was a man outside looking too unconcerned, looking a shade too thoughtfully up at the sky; and I knew Mimi was right.

"So I merely stayed with Mimi. And one day the order came. I was to go round to the chess-club that evening to receive instructions from the Grand Master. Well, I went. I had a pretty shrewd idea as to what those instructions would be. But I went.

"Well, there he was all dressed up, at the dark end of the room; dingy and curtained off, and a couple of candles.

"'You will go to Russia,' he said; and before he had time to get in another word I slipped in with what I had to say. 'Not to assassinate anybody,' I said. I slipped in with it then because, once he had given me my orders, there was an end of it. If I disobeyed after that, it was the Seine, with certain accessories: if I let him see now that I wouldn't do it for certain, there seemed the ghost of a chance. Why put themselves to the trouble of carrying a sack all the way to the Seine at night, I thought, if they knew they had nothing to gain by it? It was a slender chance. He seemed surprised, and was silent a moment. 'And if he has already signed the death-warrants of two hundred thousand innocent men and women?' he said.

"'That's his affair,' I said. 'I attend to mine.'

"'You wouldn't kill even such a man?' he said.

"'No,' I answered.

"He was silent again; so were the others; the sort of silence that seemed like earthquake, or any awful natural disaster; and the sort of robes they were wearing rustled against the silence. It was only two seconds, probably, before he spoke again.

"'I have not commanded you to assassinate anyone,' he said.

"So it worked, my slender chance.

"'You are to destroy something deadlier than a man,' he said. 'But perhaps your scruples won't let you hurt a machine?'

"The words sound simple, but he said them nastily enough.

"'I obey,' I said.

"'You will go to Russia,' he repeated. 'There is a machine in Novarsinsk that makes certain munitions. There are only three of them in Russia. They are the three deadliest machines in the world. You will wreck one of them.'

"He ceased speaking. Others gave me my passport, money, railway tickets, and a varnished walking-stick, half of which was a steel bar. I was to break off the bar later on and secrete it in my clothing, and drop it one day into the machine. And they gave me a testimonial that seemed to make me out one of the world's best experts in the handling of that particular machine, signed by some fellow that seemed to cut a good deal of ice in Russia; forged of course. I knew something of engineering, but not that much.

"'What will I do with the machine?' I asked.

"But they were busy closing down their meeting. 'You won't be there long,' said one of them, 'before you drop the bar in. Then you get back here as quickly as possible.' And he rather hustled me out. He was the man that saw me off next day, by the train across Europe. I tried to tell Mimi something about it without giving anything away. There's a lot I haven't told you: I told Mimi still less. And yet she seemed to guess a good deal of it. And the odd thing was she said I'd come back all right. Lord knows how she knew. And I remembered what she said, through the oddest experiences, and when a thousand to one against her being right looked like a safe bet to lay.

"Well I went all through Europe, past the German rye-fields, silvery green; and a great many other things; but I wasn't thinking so much of scenery, as of my chances of ever seeing it again, coming the other way. You see, I fancied I should come out of Russia by train, if I ever came out at all. You can waste your time guessing how I did come out, if you like. Certainly I never guessed it.

"Well, I arrived and showed my testimonial. It looked a good one to me when first I saw it, but nothing to what it looked to them: I was evidently just the one man in the world they were waiting for; they seemed a bit short of engineers. They brought me along to their machine; and, except that it was a machine and needed oiling, I knew very very little about it. It was a huge affair, as big as the engines of a small ship; and there it was roaring away underneath me, and they looking at it as though—well, there simply weren't any standards of comparison; they hadn't any religion, and no king, and didn't care overmuch about human life, so it's no use saying it was like one of their children to them, or a god or anything else; but I saw, from the way they looked at it, roughly what they would do to anybody that hurt it. Well, I went round oiling it, but as that was about all I was able to do for it, for a wage of £2000 a year, I thought the sooner I wrecked it and cleared out the better. And so I did. Not the clearing out; they saw to that; but the wrecking of it. I pushed the steel bar, a foot and a half of it, in through a grating with my forefinger at the end of it, with which I gave it a good send off; and it went down like an arrow in amongst the great cogs of the wheels, till a heaving piston hid it out of my sight, and it didn't heave any more, and the roar of the engine that had been like a huge purr changed its note suddenly. I didn't like that change of note coming as quick as it did. I don't know what else I expected. I see now that I might as well have tried to kill a tiger in the Zoo with a spike, and expect that none of the keepers would notice, as expect to smash a machine like that quietly. Of course I was alone when I did it, but the thing began roaring like a wounded gorilla that has been trapped in a china shop; and the Bolshies rushed in on me. Of course I said I knew nothing about it; and they didn't try to mob me. They said there would have to be a trial, and they took me to prison; but they were rather polite than otherwise. I got the idea that they would never be able to prove anything, and that my chances were quite good. What I was worrying mostly about was that they might keep me a long time in prison before they had any trial, several months perhaps; but they were in more of a hurry to deal with me than I knew. As for my chances, the first shadow came over them when one of the Russians came to the prison to question me. 'You can prove nothing whatever,' I had remarked to him.

"'Prove things!' he answered. 'We don't waste time proving things when we know perfectly well what has happened.'

"'You have to in a court of law,' I said.

"'Have to? Why?' he asked.

"'Because you might punish an innocent man otherwise,' I told him.

"He laughed rather a nasty laugh at that. 'And if we stopped the course of the law for that,' he said, 'we'd stop ploughing the steppes with our motor-tractors for fear of killing a worm.'

"I was on the point of telling him things were different in England, and stopped myself in time and did a good deal of thinking.

"And then the trial came on, very soon, as I said. I'd worked out a good enough defence. Who had ever seen me with a steel bar? How could I have concealed it? Why should I wreck a machine that was to pay me £2000 a year? And a lot more points besides. But somehow when I looked at them in their law-court I got the idea that they were up to all that. And at the very last moment I felt I must do something better.

"The charge was read out and the judge looked straight at me. 'Did you do it?' he said.

"'Yes,' I replied, on the spur of the moment.

"'Why?' he asked.

"'I was compelled to, by capitalists,' I answered.

"They were interested at once. 'Of what country?' he asked me.

"'England,' I said; and watched how the answer went down.

"'Who gave you your orders?' asked the judge.

"'The Archbishop of Canterbury,' I said, and saw that I had said the right thing. I didn't expect to get off scot-free, but if I could get the blame on to English capitalists I felt sure they would spare my life.

"'Where did he give you your orders?' said the judge.

"'At the back of his cathedral,' I answered.

"It was just right. They'd never have heard of Lambeth, and they'd have known that a secular conversation of that sort would not have gone on within the cathedral; but the shadow of its huge walls, at the back, out of the way, would have been the perfect scene for it. And they believed me too. I could see that.

"'What were his exact words?' said the judge.

"And that was where I crashed. I had nothing prepared, and with the judge's eyes on my face I had no time to prepare it now.

"'Those accursed Russians have a machine,' I began; but I saw from a change in their faces that it was no good. And one watches men's faces pretty closely when one's life hangs on what they are thinking about. You see, I hadn't liked to blackguard them too much to their faces; but my silly politeness ruined me. I should have given them the talk that they would have expected from a prominent personage of a capitalist country, instead of mincing my words as I did. Look what they had done to religion. They would have expected the archbishop to talk pretty stiffly about them, and I was altogether too mild. So all I got for trying to spare their feelings was a death sentence. I saw they had stopped believing me; and somehow, after that, my answers were merely silly. And in a minute or two the judge took a pull at his cigarette and leaned back and looked at me, then shot the smoke out of his lungs and said two words in Russian.

"'Tell him it's death,' I heard one of them say. And the sentry standing beside me, with a very nasty-looking bayonet fixed, took out his cigarette and said: 'It's death," and went on with his smoking.

"They hadn't got my real name yet, and now they asked for it, just when it seemed not to matter any longer. I gave them the name of Bourk."

"And what name do you give us?" asked Jorkens.

The man thought for a moment, and then said: "Ryan."

"This is where the tale gets a little unusual," said Jorkens to us. And the man went on.

"When they took me back to the prison, I knew I hadn't got very long. The English idea on these occasions is to give a man a little time to look after his soul; but in Russia, where you don't have one, they weren't likely to keep me waiting.

"I'd looked at the stones in my prison wall pretty thoughtfully; square grey blocks that had once had plaster over them; and now I decided to work the mortar away and get one out, after which some of the others should come more easily, and see where the hole led to. I had ten buttons on my trousers; metal ones; and by bending one of them double I got some sort of a point, and I started to scrape away the mortar at once, so as not to waste time, which was precious. The mortar came easily, being old and full of damp, and presently I began to hope. I had a chair in the cell, and I kept it handy: whenever I heard the lock in my door beginning to move I slewed the chair round and sat on it, with my back to the stone I was working on. The lock didn't move often; a man came twice a day with my food, and sometimes loafed in at an odd hour, making three times in all; but on this day he came in once oftener, attracted, I suppose, by the interesting news that they had condemned me to death. I always had my chair in place by the time the key had turned, and was sitting on it before the door began to open. By nightfall I had the stone loose, and had only used two buttons, and even they were by no means finished. That night I got it out, and worked till dawn on one of the stones behind it; then I tidied up the dust, eating some of it, and put the stone back, and had some sleep for an hour or two. But I didn't want to waste much time on sleep, as I didn't know how long I'd got; and early that morning I was at work again, this time on the next stone. And I was getting along splendidly.

"They are devils. They know how to make you despair. I had never despaired in all my life before. I had held back from despair as you keep from the brink of a precipice. But those Russians brought me to it. They must have been watching me through some spy-hole they had; for the lock turned and one of them came in, and there was I sitting comfortably in my chair with my back to the loose stones, and the bent bit of button in my pocket. And he never said a word. Just threw a hammer and a good sharp chisel down on the floor in front of me and walked out of the cell. Then I knew that those walls must be about ten feet thick, and that nothing was any good, and I left the hammer and chisel where they had fallen and gave myself up to despair. If he had put me into a lower dungeon, or manacled me, or flogged me, I could have held out against it, but that hammer and chisel somehow or other seemed the very last notes of doom.

"The man that came in with my food just looked at the chisel, as you might take a look at a snake, just to see that I wasn't near enough to use it on him; then he left it and the hammer lying there.

"Next day I was sitting there hopeless, when in walked another fellow, a good deal neater than the rest. I looked up.

"'Do you want a reprieve?' he said.

"But I had seen the look on his face. I don't know what I thought he was going to ask for; to betray all those people in Paris, I suppose. But the look on his face was enough, and I said: 'No thank you.'

"'Not want a reprieve?' he asked.

"'No, not today, thank you,' I answered.

"'If it's not today, you'll not want it at all,' he said. 'You're for the cellar tomorrow morning.'

"And he hung about near the door, to see if I'd change my mind. But I wouldn't. I felt sure that there must be some crab in it, from the look I had seen on his face.

"Well, a little while later another man came in, as though the first hadn't come in at all.

"'I've got a reprieve for you,' he said.

"'What have I got to do for it?' I asked him.

"'We want to explore a distant place; perhaps to colonize it,' he said. 'We want you to go there first, and light a fire as a sign when you get there.'

"'What else?' I asked.

"'Nothing else,' he said.

"'How do I get there?' said I.

"'We send you,' he said.

"'Where is it?' I asked.

"'The moon,' he replied.

"'Nonsense,' I said.

"'Yes, to capitalists,' he answered. 'They're all two hundred years behind Russia; and imperialism is as far as they can think. But the moon is well within the scope of our scientists.'

"'How would you get me there?' I asked.

"'Shoot you out of a gun,' he said.

"'Well, there's two reasons why you couldn't do that,' I told him.

"'Well?' he said with a superior smile.

"'Firstly,' I said, 'the thing would smash to fragments on landing; or more likely melt.'

"'There's a parachute that you can release from a spring inside,' he said, 'as soon as you see you're close. The head of the shell is crystal.'

"'Well, there's another reason,' I said. 'Starting off at a thousand feet per second would merely finish one. Why, even a railway train . . .'

"'You don't,' he said. 'You're moving at three to four hundred miles an hour when you enter the gun.'

"'How do you manage that?' I asked.

"Always the slow superior smile, as though their scientists were all grown up and the people in other countries only children.

"'We've rails,' he said, 'and the shell is on very low wheels. It runs on those rails over what is almost a precipice, four or five hundred feet of it, and that's how it gets its pace. The moment it enters the tunnel a steel door falls behind it. The tunnel's the gun. As in any gun, the near end, the chamber, is larger, and the powder is stacked there all round you; but when you get to the barrel it exactly fits the shell, even to a groove for the wheels. The powder is ignited behind you the moment you pass, slow-burning big blocks of black powder, slow-burning I mean when compared with modern explosives, and by the time you leave the muzzle you have your maximum speed. Is that simple enough for you?'

"'Is the gun rifled?' I asked.

"Again the smile, as though he spoke to a child. 'Of course,' he said. 'The grooves for the wheels are twisted round the barrel.'

"'Then the spin will addle my brains,' I said, 'and I shan't unloose any parachute.'

"'There's a gyroscope in your cabin,' he answered.

"'What? The outside spins, while the gyroscope holds the cabin?'

"'Of course,' he said.

"'And what will I breathe?' I asked.

"'Oxygen,' he replied.

"'And eat and drink?'

"'We give you supplies,' said he.

"'And how long will they last on the moon?' I asked.

"'We'll send over more shells,' he said.

"'Supposing one of them hits me,' I said.

"'Very unlikely,' he answered. 'Whereas our man in the cellar was working hard all through the busy time, perhaps fifty thousand cases, and he's never missed yet.'

"I could see they were pretty keen for me to go, from that tactful reference to the swine in the cellar. Well, I wasn't keen on the cellar, and I accepted. A bit longer to live, and that was to the good, and any way I would get out of Russia.

"They released me from the prison and housed me decently; as a matter of fact there was tapestry all over the walls; but it wasn't any easier to escape; they saw to that all right. There was a court-yard all round the palace in which they kept me, and a thirty-foot wall beyond, and plenty of soldiers walking about between.

"What they were keenest on was my lighting a fire when I got there: they gave me a packet of powder to spread over a hundred yards square, and they were going to watch with their telescopes. They were keen on Russia being the first to do it, and keen on proving they had. Any Russians that they could spare they had probably killed already, so they had to send people like me. If I lit the fire they would send other men after me; if I didn't, they would send over no more provisions. They fed me well, very well indeed; in fact they seemed as fond of me as a farmer is of a good fat turkey when it is getting near Christmas. They took me out and showed me their apparatus; a huge high iron scaffold on a hill, with a lift running up it, and the rails running airily down over a flimsy viaduct, and their long steel tunnel lying along the fields, slanting very slightly upwards, just enough for the shell to clear the low hills in the West on its way to the new moon. New, you see, so that it would most of it be in darkness and they would be able to see my fire. And there was the shell all ready, waiting at the end of its rail. And they opened it and showed me my bunk inside, like the smallest berth on a boat you ever saw; barely room to turn round; a nasty place to spend ten days or a fortnight. And the gadgets they showed me too, the oxygen gas-mask for use on the moon, and the switch for releasing the parachute that was to steady the shell before landing. When it came to the switch for the parachute I pointed out that there wasn't much air on the moon. 'Not much,' said one of them, the same man that first offered me the reprieve; 'but we have evidence that there is some. Four or five hundred feet would be all you'd want for the parachute,' brushing aside lightly enough what was probably the principal drawback. I bet he'd have worried more about that air if he'd been the one that was going.

"Then we went down and had a look at the tunnel, with its steel door up in the air like a guillotine, the door that was to fall behind me the moment the shell ran in, and would close the breech of the gun. We walked in and saw the big blocks of black powder lying beside the rails and stacked round the walls, and then the sudden narrowing of the tunnel.

"'The bigger the blocks of powder the slower they burn,' said my friend, if one can use such a word of the man who had sneeringly offered reprieve. 'The explosion gradually increases in force all the time you are in the gun.'

"I may say that that moon-shooting tunnel was over two hundred yards long.

"There seemed sense in what they told me about the gun, but I couldn't get over my fear that the lunar atmosphere would be too thin for the parachute, and that I should crash through it and melt on landing. I watched them talking among themselves in the tunnel and knew what they were saying, though I didn't know Russian: they were boasting that the U.S.S.R. would do it.

"'It's a thousand to one against getting there,' I blurted out to the man who talked English.

"'Russia will do it,' he answered. 'Our scientists don't leave things to prayer or chance, like the people in capitalist countries. If it's a thousand to one we'll send a thousand men, and get one there, and then a thousand more, and as many thousands as we need to get enough there to colonize it.'

"So that was the sort of men they were.

"Well, there seemed nothing for it but to try to live as long as I could. 'Will you give me a fortnight's holiday before I start?' I said.

"And to my surprise they said Yes. Well, next day Eisen called for me rather early; that's what the sneering man called himself, the man whose reprieve I'd refused; and he said that he wanted to show me all over the shell again, so that I should know all about it, and that after that we'd go to a theatre, and to a dance with some girls he knew. He talked of the girls all the way to the high gaunt tower, and they really seemed very nice. One in particular, he said, would be very glad to meet me: he knew her tastes. He said this just as I got inside the shell; he had been describing her all the way up in the lift. The moon, a little past full, was high in the sky behind us as I got in, the long gun pointing away from it. Eisen put his hand in and began showing me things; then he questioned me about everything in the shell, because he said that I had to know all about it before I went on my holiday, and he kept on explaining about spreading the powder on a hundred yards square on the moon. 'She's a very pretty one, that girl,' he said all of a sudden. Then he showed me how the door shut.

"There was a grinding of wheels at once. Lord! we were off! I thought at first that it was an accident, but I've found that, however easily people fool you, you find it out when you think it over, some-times long afterwards. Having the moon behind me was one thing that helped to fool me. It never occurred to me that the gun might be aiming at just where the moon would be ten days to a fortnight later, when the shell would be due to arrive. Well, it was a sickening feeling, dropping down the rails from that tower. I lay there on the sort of bed, wondering when we'd come to the tunnel. As a matter of fact I remember nothing of that. It was all very well for them to talk of the increase of speed being gradual, but somewhere or other in that tunnel I must have had a jolt that was a bit too much for my brains; for I opened my eyes feeling very sleepy indeed, and when I remem-bered what had been happening and looked out through the crystal window, there was nothing but sky in sight.

"That damned Russian had turned on the oxygen, or I wouldn't have been alive. How many hours or days had passed since leaving earth I had no idea, nor any idea how far we were away from it. Nor could I see the moon. All I knew was that I was rushing through space at the pace of a bullet, and all I felt was the most absolute stillness, the most absolute stillness that I have ever known; and no sound but the purr of my gyroscope that was keeping my cabin steady while the shell rotated. No sound of any wind or the passage of air; so I knew I was outside Earth's atmosphere. An intolerable glitter oppressed me, a glare still and unflickering, sunlight rushing through space unhindered by clouds or air. I shut my eyes to escape it, but could not sleep; and so hours went by. And then a shadow came over us that I felt through my closed eyes, and I looked through the crystal again, and at once the stars came out. This blessed shadow wrapped us for half an hour, and passed away again and the glare returned."

"What made the shadow?" I asked.

And Ryan looked up wearily from his absinthe, weary still, it seemed, from the memory of that long journey, unsheltered in sunlight: "Sunset," he said, "and then in half an hour it came up on the other side. We were as far as that from Earth."

"How awful," I couldn't help saying.

"But I was out of Russia," he said. "Still I couldn't see the moon. I didn't know where I was, or how long we'd been going. I ate some food: I didn't know how many hours or days I had been without it; and I drank some water, and it tasted good. And then a curious thing happened. I'd been lying back in my bunk, facing the way we were going, with my feet a lot higher than my head."

"You should never sleep like that," said Jorkens.

"No," replied Ryan, "and it probably helped to keep me unconscious much longer than I should have been otherwise. But I don't know. But now I was sliding down more and more to the other end, and pressing against my feet. The head of the shell had been higher than its base, and was now evidently lower. I drank a lot more water during the next few hours, which I seemed to want more than food; and nothing else changed. And then my bed seemed to be a little steeper, and I was pressing a little harder against my feet. And suddenly through the crystal head of the shell the weary steely glitter disappeared, and a soft grey took its place. The relief to the eye, and the brain itself, was immense. But I had no idea where I was, or what was happening. And then sound came again, the sound of what could only be air. And the soft grey darkened. It came to me with extraordinary suddenness, and nearly too late, that it was time to use the parachute. It worked, and there was a bump that broke the end of my bed. We had landed. The first thing I did was to slip on the oxygen gas-mask, that they had given me to wear when walking about on the Moon. I could see nothing at all, for most of the crystal nose of the shell was buried, and the rest of it was all blurred, with some atmospheric disturbance that looked like rain. Then I opened the door that Eisen had shut in Russia, and walked out wearing my gas-mask; and sure enough it was rain, and it splashed on my eye-pieces and dimmed them at once, and it seemed to be evening. From a soft patch of soil in which we had luckily landed I stepped at once on an expanse that I could feel rather than see to be utterly devoid of all vegetation. In fact it was exactly the sandy or gravelly waste that I had expected to find by the shore of some dried-up lunar sea. But our anticipations do not always guide us aright; for suddenly just behind me I heard the words: 'Are you aware you are trespassing?'

"Yes, it was England. England all over. And a man who couldn't have been either a Russian or an inhabitant of the moon came towards me, looking at me out of his eye-glass, along his gravel drive. My shell had landed in one of his flower-beds, and the parachute draped all over it looked like a fallen tent. Well, I'm not a lunatic. So I didn't say to him: 'I have come out of a gun in Russia, but I was looking for the moon.' No, I said: 'I'm very sorry, sir, but I'm down from London, camping; and I didn't know it was private. I'll go away at once.' He gave one disgusted look at his flower-bed, and went away with his nose in the air. You see I'd told him exactly what he'd expected, as when I told the Russians about the Archbishop of Canterbury, and there was no more for him to say. Well, I didn't like to leave that shell for the Press of the world to write about. I was none too sure I mightn't get extradited over that business of the steel bar. So I got hold of the powder that was to light up the moon, and mixed it with everything inflammable in the shell and put the oxygen canisters on top of it; and, protecting it all from the rain with the parachute, I set the whole thing alight. It made a fine glow in the sky; but they wouldn't have seen that in Russia: they were looking for it in the wrong place. And I doubt if what was left of the shell, after that, got into even the local papers. And by the evening of the next day I saw Mimi again, as she had told me I would."

"Now, you know, that's unusual," said Jorkens to Tutton and me. "I should say distinctly unusual."

The Club Secretary

I think I have said that it is the custom in our Club to discuss gardening during the spring and summer, or rather to hear the tales of what various members have been doing in their gardens, or of any wonderful growth that has come unwontedly early or incredibly large in the garden of any one of us; but when the season of fogs returns, and the sun sets behind houses before the middle of luncheon, it is rather our custom to tell tales of brighter scenes, to keep our little crescent before the fire from falling asleep, or from drifting away one by one to toy with some tedious business. It was upon such an occasion as this that one of our group in his chair before the fire, who seemed about to be falling asleep, suddenly opened his eyes wide and exclaimed: "For the Lord's sake someone tell us of somewhere where there is sunlight." And I heard Jorkens draw in a breath. But, before he had time to speak, the voice of Terbut was raised. "And let's hear of England this time," he said. "I'm tired of the ends of the earth."

A more deliberate attempt to put Jorkens out of his stride I have seldom heard. But it had no effect. "I saw a curious thing once in England," Jorkens said; "a very curious thing. I was taking a walk out of London once—a long walk with sandwiches, and a good flask, one that would hold a pint. Partly I went for exercise, but it was more to please the spirit than the body that I went. I had somehow got tired of pavements. You know how one feels then; and Spring was coming on with a rush. I don't know what way I went, only that it must have been roughly southwards, for the sun was in my eyes, until it got round to my right.

"I started early and had no lunch until some time after two, for I would not sit down and eat till I was completely clear of London. I must have done a good twenty miles. I sat myself down on a bank of grass by the road, with a hedge in front of me as green as a meteor, along the top of a bank on the opposite side. Primroses were out on the bank, and early violets. There I ate my lunch, with birds singing, and white clouds scurrying over the dome of a blue sky. What was the other side of the hedge on the bank I had no idea: I could see neither through nor over. I sat there wondering comfortably all through my lunch. And after lunch my long walk, the bright sun, birds singing, and one thing and another, were bringing a drowsiness on me, when a sudden bout of curiosity made me leap up and cross the road, and look for a gap in the hedge. Through a gap low down among the stems of the thorn I saw smooth lawns stretching away, and a little house with bow windows and bottle-glass panes and red roof, that was clearly the house of a golf club. And looking at it through the hedge never soothed my curiosity, for the light of Spring was hanging so strongly over those lawns that they somehow seemed to have the glow of lawns seen long ago in the early morning and remembered almost from infancy; there seemed something as magical about them as that.

"I was a lot slenderer in those days, and once I got my head through the gap in the hedge it was only a matter of wriggling. No one was playing golf, and I walked up to the clubhouse with not a soul in sight, and no sound of anyone stirring. Grass of Parnassus was flowering in such abundance that I wondered if those smooth lawns were not too marshy for golf. I came all in the silence to the oaken door of the golf club. And there a hall-porter, glittering with livery that was out of date in its splendour, opened the door at once. I had then to apologize and explain I was lost; and, thinking to put a better face on it to an official of the club than to the hall-porter, or at any rate hoping to gain time, I asked to see the secretary. Well, the secretary was in the little clubhouse, and the hall-porter brought him at once.

"'What can I do for you?' he said, all amiability.

"'I wanted to apologize,' I said. 'I am not a member of your golf club. I lost my way on your links.'

"He smiled away my apology. 'It's not a golf club,' he said.

"'Not?' said I.

"'No,' he replied airily. Why did I say 'airily?' He seemed to me airy. He seemed volatile, energetic, even for a club secretary. 'No, not a golf club,' he said.

"'I quite thought it was a golf club,' said I.

"'No,' he replied. 'It's a club, as a matter of fact, for poets.'

"'For poets?' I said.

"'Yes,' said the secretary, 'and, what may quite surprise you, for the poets of all time.'

"'Of all time?' I said.

"'Yes,' he repeated, and, beckoning me forward to the inner doors of the hall, he pointed through its glass panes. 'There you see Swinburne,' he said, 'talking to Herrick.'

"And sure enough I recognized the earnest face of Swinburne talking, and saw the man that the secretary told me was Herrick giving little answering chuckles. And somehow, in spite of what the secretary had said, it didn't surprise me at all; there was something so fairy-like in the light on the lawns before I got to the club, and something so far from this age in the little house, that it seemed only natural that it had gathered up from the ages what was lost to other lawns. I should not have been surprised to see Homer himself. And sure enough there he stood, stroking his beard, eyes full of thought, giving me somehow the impression of a most tremendous Tory.

"'And there's Stephen Phillips,' he said, 'talking to Dante.'

"And I recognized the two men, and seemed to see, through the rather dim glass of the door, a certain resemblance of feature.

"'A bit lucky, wasn't he, getting elected?' I said, pointing to Stephen Phillips.

"'Well, yes,' said the secretary, 'but you have luck in all clubs—there's always somebody who may be just not quite.'

"And then Tennyson went by, on the other side of the shimmering glass. I recognized him immediately.

"'He's having a bit of a slump over there,' I said, pointing over the lawns to the way by which I had come.

"'Oh, he's all right here,' said the secretary.

"'And the waiters?' I said, for they were passing to and fro.

"'All writers too,' he said. 'All wrote good stuff. But not immortal. He's the best we have on our staff,' he said, pointing to the hall-porter. 'That's Pope.'

"'Pope,' I said. 'Is it really? I suppose your standard of member-ship . . .'

"'Pretty high,' he said. 'You see, we have Shakespeare, Milton, and all of them. There goes Shelley.'

"And sure enough I saw a light figure slipping by, to drop what looked like a political pamphlet unnoticed in somebody's hat.

"'And the name of the club?' I asked.

"'The Elysian Club,' he said.

"Somehow I had thought so.

"Pope only hall-porter, Homer himself a member. Who, then, was the secretary? That was the question which in this extraordinary club, where I might have found so much of overpowering interest, became the one thought that absorbed me. What a power is curiosity, when once awakened! I might have heard Shakespeare speak. And yet I wasted my time in trying to satisfy my miserable curiosity as to who the secretary was.

"'Of course you write yourself,' I said.

"'Very little,' he answered; 'I gave it up long ago.'

"Gave it up! That was even more baffling than ever. Yet greater than Pope, whoever he was. Was he Keats? I thought for a moment. For Keats perhaps wrote little compared to some of them. But no, Keats never gave it up.

"There was nothing for it but to ask him his name. Which I did. And he told me. And, do you know, it conveyed to me nothing whatever. And that was awkward. It left me saying, 'Yes, yes, of course,' and remarks like that, too transparent not to be seen through. But he took no offence. 'No, no, you wouldn't have heard of me,' he said. 'I never wrote enough. One great line—that's what the members say. If I had written thirty I could have been a member myself. But only one great line, they say. Better than that fellow, you know,' he said, pointing to the hall-porter. 'Yet not enough for full membership. But I am an honorary member.'

"Well, I've read a good deal of poetry, knocking about the world, and the line might convey something where the name never could. And sure enough it did. I asked him if he would mind repeating the line to me; and he began at once. 'A rose-red,' he began, but I got the rest of it in before he had time to. 'City half as old as time,' said I.

"'Yes,' he said. 'A rose-red city half as old as time,' repeating the beautiful line like a good host relishing a taste of his century-old port. 'It's a pity I couldn't have made thirty of them; but I am really very comfortable as I am. Would you like to see my office?'

"Well, he showed me into a very snug little room, and I should have liked to stop and talk with him, and especially to see more of the members; but, after all, I had forced my way into the club, and had taken up quite enough of his time already. So I offered him my pint flask, which of course I had filled with whiskey, as some slight return for his trouble. And, do you know, he drank up every drop of it. When I opened it for a drop for myself when I got back to the road, I found it was quite empty."

A Mystery of the East

November had come round again, and the woods away beyond London were a glory, and London had drawn round her ancient shoulders the grey cloak she wears at this season. It was dim in the room at the club where we sat after lunch, the curtains round the one window seemed tall masses of shadow, and we were talking about the mystery of the East. It was really more than mystery we were discussing; for one who had met it in Port Said, another in Aden, a third who believed he had seen it in Kilindini, and a collector of butterflies who had met it all over India, were telling tales of pure magic. It is my object in recording tales I hear at my club to relate only those that are true so far as we know, and that seem to me to be interesting, but none of these stories of magic fulfilled either of these conditions, and I do not therefore retell them; yet I mention them because they gradually woke Jorkens, who happened to be asleep, and drew from him what is to me a very interesting statement.

"They understand magic perfectly," he asserted.

"What? Who do?" we said, startled by the vehement statement from the man that we thought was still sleeping.

"The East," said Jorkens. "I mean to say those in the East whose business it is. Just as one says that the West understands machinery. Of course you'd find millions in Europe who could not run a machine, but engineers can."

"And in the East?" I said, to keep him to the point.

"In the East," said Jorkens, "the magicians understand magic."

"Can you give us a case in point?" asked Terbut. And I'm glad he did, for one often hears of the mystery of the East, but seldom, as now, a definite story of magic, with every detail that anybody could ask for.

"Certainly I can," replied Jorkens, now wide awake.

I have little doubt that Terbut hoped, in a tale of magic, to catch Jorkens out with something he could not prove, more thoroughly than he could ever hope to catch him over some more solid tale of travel or sport. How completely he failed I leave the reader to judge.

And then Jorkens began his story.

"On a bank of the Ganges, not so long ago, I was standing looking at that pearl of a river; there flowed the water of it a yard or two from my feet, and there flowed the beauty of it right through me. It was evening, and river and sky were not only unearthly, as you might suppose, but they somehow seemed realler than earth, with a reality that all the while was growing and growing and growing. So that if ever I had left the world we know for the world of fancies and song that seems sometimes to drift so near to it, then is the time I'd have gone. But I was brought back suddenly to reality by stepping on to a man who was sitting beside the river, while my gaze was far off in the twilight. In fact I fell over him, and all light of the Ganges was gone clean out of my mind; but he still sat motionless there with his eyes as full of the beauty of river and sky as they had probably been for hours. That is, I suppose, one of the principal differences between us and people like that; we can probably appreciate the glory of such a river under that sort of sky, with the fires of the burning-ghats beginning to glow, and a young moon floating slender over their temples, we can probably appreciate it almost as well as they can; but we don't seem able to cling to it. Well, as I was saying, I was brought back to earth in every sense of the word, and there was this man, naked above the waist, sitting as though; well, there's only one way to describe it; sitting as though I had not been there at all. One of those what-d'you-call-'ems, I said to myself. And all of a sudden the idea came to test him."

"How did you do that?" asked Terbut.

"Nothing simpler," said Jorkens. "Well, in one way it wasn't so simple, because I had to explain to him what a sweepstake was, and what numbers were, in fact practically everything; and I don't suppose he really understood; but one thing I did make him understand, and that was that the number on a ticket that I showed him was the same as the number on a ticket in another part of the world, and that it was his job to make that other ticket come first out of a drum, first among millions. I got him to understand that, because he asked me why, and I told him that there was money on it. When a man starts asking questions you can nearly always make him understand, because you can see just where he has stuck, and can help him on every time. So he said that he had not the power to make the money of use to me, and I said: 'Never you mind about that.' And the rest he promised to do. The ticket with that very number should come first of all out of the drum, or there was no power in Ganges. And then he took my ticket out of my hand and held it up high in that glow of sunset and small moon and fires, and gave it back and went on with his meditation. I wanted to thank him, but it was no use whatever; his spirit was somewhere far off: I might as well have tried to talk to one of his

Indian gods.

"Well, I may as well tell you that that sweepstake was to be worth £30,000; and I walked away pretty pleased, for I could see that if there is anything whatever in magic, or whatever it is that these people practise, then I was sure of the prize; he had given his word for that. Of course I still thought that there might possibly be nothing in it; but, if there was, there could be no possible doubt that he was one of them, or that he had exerted his power just as he said.

"Well, I left the Ganges next day; I left India within the week; and you may imagine I was pretty full of my chances of getting £30,000. Was there anything in the mystery of the East or was there not? That was the point. Now there was a man in the ship who knew, if anyone knew, a man called Lupton. He knew the East as well as anyone born on this side of the world is likely to know it; and, in particular, he knew about this very thing; I mean magic. Unfortunately I'd never met him, and I hardly liked to go up and beard him, he was too distinguished for that; and there was I watching him walking by me every day, and knowing that he carried the secret of my £30,000, the simple knowledge of whether or not the East could do what it claimed. Well, sooner or later on board a ship you get to know everybody, though we were into the Mediterranean before I was introduced to him; and almost the first thing I said to him was, 'Is there anything in this magic that they say they can do in the East?'

"It very nearly shut him up altogether, for he thought that I was speaking of magic lightly. But he luckily saw I was serious. I suppose he saw some light from that thirty thousand that there must have been in my eyes. For after a moment's silence, as though he were not going to answer, he turned and, speaking in a quite friendly way, said: 'You might, just as well, doubt wireless.'

"So then I asked him what I wanted to know: was it possible for a man to exert any influence in the East that could cause a ticket to come first out of a drum in Dublin? And I remember still the very words of his answer: 'Is it a very rare power,' he said; 'yet not only can it be done, but I know a man now living who is able to do it.'

"Well, I asked him then about my friend by the Ganges, but he knew nothing about him. His man lived in North Africa. My man might be able to do it too, he said, but there were very few of them. There was one obvious crab in the situation, and a difficult one to deal with: why didn't he go to his African friend himself, and lift that thirty thousand? He was a distinguished man and I'd only just been introduced to him, and it wasn't too easy a question to ask. But I managed it. Of course my question was all wrapped up, but I got it out. And he answered me quite sincerely. 'I'm settling down now near London,' he said, 'on my pension and what I've put by, and I don't say that if anyone offered me thirty thousand I shouldn't be grateful to him; only, living as much in the East as I have done, one has taken a good deal of quinine in one's time, and in the end it's bad for the nerves; and if I got thirty thousand like that, out of the East by magic, I'd always be worrying as to whether the East might get level. I know it's silly of me, but there it is. You probably don't feel like that.'

"'No, I don't think I do,' I said. I couldn't say any more, for fear of hurting his feelings. But thirty thousand, you know; and afraid that the East might try to get it back! Well, let the East try: that was all I felt about it. But first of all let's get it. So I said, 'What part of North Africa were you saying that this man lived in?'

"He smiled at my persistence, and told me. 'Not very far in,' he said. 'A night and half a day by train from the coast. You had better get out at El Kántara; and a few days ride on a mule from there will bring you to the Ouled Naïl Mountains, where he lives.'

"'What part of the mountains?' I asked. For he had stopped speaking, and a mountain range seemed rather an incomplete address.

"'Oh, there's no difficulty in finding him,' he said. 'He's a holy man, and well enough known. You merely ask one of the nomads for Hamid ben Ibrahim, when you get to the feet of the mountains. Besides, you can see his house for twenty miles. It's only ten foot high, and about eight yards broad and long; but it's white-washed, under brown mountains, and the desert is flat in front of it all the way to the Niger. You'll find Hamid all right.'

"'They don't all do it for nothing, I suppose,' said I; 'like my friend on the Ganges.'

"You see, I hadn't very much cash in hand after my trip to India, not counting my hope of the thirty thousand pounds.

"'No,' he said. 'But he'll do it for this.'

"And he gave me a little packet out of his pocket; a powder, as I could feel through the paper.

"'What is it?' I said.

"'Bismuth,' he answered. 'His digestion's bad. But he's too holy to take an aperient; never has had one in his life, or smoked; and of course brandy is out of the question. So he is rather hard to cure. As you probably know, all Europeans are held to be doctors over there; so the first thing he'll do is to tell you his symptoms and ask you to cure him; and I think bismuth may do it. If it does, he'll work that ticket for you. In fact he knows a good deal more about magic than any of us know of medicine. And you might ask the ship's doctor for anything else that might be good for him. He's pretty fat, and takes no exercise. Do what you can for the old fellow.'

"'I certainly will,' I said. It seemed only fair.

"'And I should buy a tent in Algiers,' he said, 'rather than hire one from an Arab. You'll find it will cost you about a quarter as much. Or an eighth. It depends how good you are at bargaining.'

"Daylight had gone while we talked, without my noticing it; and I looked up and saw bands of stars where there had been scarlet and gold. And a chill came with the stars, and Lupton's face went grey; for the chill after sunset seemed the one thing he was unable to stand, though you'd have thought the opposite, living as he had lived, more in tents than in houses. So he went below, and his last words to me were: 'He can do it all right. You need have no doubt of that.'

"Well, I troubled Lupton no more; oddly enough I rather avoided him, for any conversation we might have had would have sounded so trivial after this mystery of the East that he had revealed to me, while all those millions of stars slipped softly out to shine in the Mediterranean. And before the end of the week we came to Marseilles. Well, I got out there. If I'd gone on to England I'd only have had to come back again, in order to get to Africa; and the finances wouldn't have run to it. My only difficulty was how to get another ticket in that sweepstake, as I didn't want the two spells working on the same ticket; but, do you know, I was able to buy one from a man in Marseilles, who seemed to have lost faith in his luck. So with that I slipped across to Algiers by a line that goes backwards and forwards from Marseilles to the African coast, and cheers itself against any monotony it may find in that by calling itself the Compagnie Générale Transatlantique. I hadn't entirely lost faith in my friend by the Ganges; I had kept his ticket and wanted to see what he could do; but naturally, after having that talk with one of the foremost orientalists, I relied a great deal more on the man he had recommended me. When first I had seen the man by the Ganges it had hardly seemed possible to me that he could fail, so overpowering seemed his eyes, and so much his spirit seemed dwelling only temporarily in that body that sat by the river, and able to exert its power on one place as well as another. But now I was all under the influence of Lupton, and only wanted to find the man in the Ouled Naïl Mountains.

"Well, I bought a cheap tent in Algiers and took the train one evening, and the next afternoon I came in sight of the mountains, going up like spires from El Kántara. There I told the Arabs that I was a doctor, travelling to the desert in search of health. It was easy enough for them to believe me, for I had given proof of medical knowledge by that very remark; for, do you know, there is more health in the Sahara than in the whole length of Harley Street. But in any case it was perfectly true what Lupton had told me, that every European is credited, in those parts, with being a doctor. But I was a very special kind of doctor, and I had brought a few aperients and some extra quinine in order to prove it further. One day, with the wind in the date palms under those barren precipices, I started off on mules with three Arabs, riding south-westwards. Somehow El Kántara always reminds me of gold in iron vaults, the green mass of a thousand date-palms, these people's only wealth, and all round them rocks that have never known as much green as you sometimes see on a salt-cellar."

"You were telling us," I said, "of the man you were looking for in the Ouled Naïl Mountains."

"I beg your pardon," said Jorkens. "Yes, we were riding south-westwards. As soon as we got through the pass we were in the desert, and we rode keeping the mountains on our right. We were never far from water: old torrents that had come with storms in the mountains had scooped out hundreds of basins in all the dry ravines; and over every one you came to someone had placed a flat stone, to protect the water that lay there from being drunk up by the sun. We had an easy journey, camping whenever the mules were tired; and as we ambled past the flocks of the nomads the rumour of my skill as a doctor went on swiftly before me. Ah, those evenings in the desert, with the afterglow on the mountains; and here it's all dark and noisy and full of houses."

"You found the Ouled Naïl Mountains?" I said.

"Ah, yes," said Jorkens. "Yes, yes, of course. We kept out in the desert, and one day there was the whole range of them lying on our right. We kept out in the desert till I saw the white house. I saw it suddenly one evening. There had been no sign of anything on the mountains; and then the sun set, and far away to the north-east of us, I saw the house stand out exactly as Lupton described it, with its door and its two small windows, miles and miles away.

"I moved into the mountains to get water next day; and then I said that I had found the health that I sought and would go back to El Kántara, and we went along under the mountains, on a course that brought me close to the little house. Of course we and our mules were visible from the house on the rocks all the morning, and my reputation as a physician had arrived there long before, so that as soon as I drew near, the holy man came running out of his house, so far as a man of that shape may be said to be able to run. Well, I talked a good deal of Arabic, of a sort, and he talked a good deal of bad French, and we understood one another perfectly. Diagnosis is always a good thing in medicine, as any doctor will tell you, but it is particularly effective when you are able to do it before the patient has spoken at all. You see, I knew all about this man from Lupton. So I told him all his symptoms. And then I gave him some medicine right away, and he made some coffee for me and we sat and talked for five hours. Whether it was the medicine or the diagnosis, he was feeling better already, and when it came to offering me some fee I told him that my skill to heal was rather the result of magic than the study of medicine, and that therefore I took no fee; but that if, as some rumour among the nomads rather seemed to have indicated, he was himself a brother magician, I should be well content to be shown a little of his own magic; and I brought out the ticket I had bought in Marseilles from the man who had given up faith in it.

"He looked at the number of the ticket, and understood the whole thing at once, very unlike the man on the Ganges. Yes; he could do it. And I wouldn't have taken an offer then of twenty thousand pounds for that ticket.

"And he was right; he could do it. Lupton was right. There's magic in the East of which we know nothing.

"I went back to El Kántara then, back to London, third class of course all the way, and put those two tickets in a bank, and waited for the draw in the lottery."

"But wait a moment," said Terbut. "You say he could do it."

"Certainly," said Jorkens. "And the man by the Ganges too."

"Then you got sixty thousand pounds," said Terbut; "not only thirty."

"Well, read for yourself," said Jorkens. "I kept the cutting to this day." And he took a cutting from an Irish paper out of an old leather wallet he had. He gave it to Terbut, and Terbut read it aloud. "At the fateful moment," he read, "a hundred nurses paraded before the drum, dressed as early-Victorian bicyclists, and marched past Mr. O'Riotty, who took the salute, attended by two machine-guns. A door in the drum was then opened, and the first nurse put in her hand to bring out the fortunate number. She accidentally brought out two tickets, and Mr. O'Riotty ordered them both to be put back."

"You needn't read any further," said Jorkens.

"What?" said Terbut.

"No," replied Jorkens. "The mistake I made. The mistake I made," he repeated. "Oh, but of course it's easy to see it now."

"I see," began Terbut thoughtfully. "You think that both of them . . ."

But Jorkens only let out an impatient gasp.

"Never mind," I said. "Have a whiskey."

"A whiskey!" said Jorkens. "What is the use of that?"

The remark staggered me. It seemed to me to mark one of those changes that come suddenly in a man's life, like a milestone flashing upon a rapid traveller, and that bring to a close some period of his story. With what more momentous event could I close this book?